DIVIDED STATES

Willow River Press is an imprint of Between the Lines Publishing. The Willow River Press name and logo are trademarks of Between the Lines Publishing.

Cover by: Morgan Bliadd

Between the Lines Publishing
1769 Lexington Ave N, Ste 286
Roseville MN 55113
btwnthelines.com

First Published: June 2025

ISBN: (Paperback) 978-1-965059-46-3

ISBN: (Ebook) 978-1-965059-47-0

Library of Congress Control Number: 2025936382

DIVIDED STATES

BOB THOMAS

As always, my wife Molly

Part I:

Dissolution – The Fall of the Empire

Prologue

Though the events described within this story happened years ago, their impact continues to be felt. Massive changes occurred within a relatively short period of time. This Prologue recounts the conditions that existed and enabled all that subsequently occurred.

Life in the United States

The year was slowly ending with a holiday season that started around Thanksgiving and extended through the New Year. In the northeast corner of the United States, darkness arrived at 5:00 pm with the only light being the harsh white glare of streetlamps. In this silent, energy-less outdoor world, the small windows of nearby high-rise office complexes remained fully lit with many employees completing last-minute projects in anticipation of the holiday ahead. Though their minds had already left for the day, their bodies remained behind – everyone needing the work and unable to afford to skip out early for fear of becoming unemployed. With jobs increasingly scarce within the United States, employees had to defensively preserve positions already held – lacking the luxury of any hope to improve themselves.

The country had become a divisive place of extremes. While some chose to sit back and wait for the world to change, others became survivalists by preparing for the worst - gathering and hiding supplies. The United States President – a five-term incumbent – was the nexus of all controversy – suppressing opposing opinions, restricting freedom of movement, and inciting crowds to a frenzy. Some people loved him; others hated him. However, everyone had an opinion about polarizing President King.

The single word that best describes these times is unstable – applying to both King and the world he created. As a result, everyone had become fearful . . . afraid to lose jobs . . . afraid to be outspoken. While people received plenty of essential services delivered in a timely, efficient way, such benefits were just limited to the basic necessities, not frivolous enjoyment.

Life in the United States was clearly not perfect, but many feared their lives could get far worse.

Uncle Sam's Big Brother (Or – Someone is Always Watching)

Once a typical workday was done, the lights in those tall buildings would gradually go dark as person after person exited the office with red lights blinking as security cards got swiped . . . and then turned green. Ten steps later, the card would get swiped again upon entering a nearby drugstore and again upon leaving and boarding a bus. Red-green-red-green-red—on and on ad infinitum as the same drill got repeated a half dozen more times by thousands of people in hundreds of communities as everyone began their slow treks home. This world was one of hurry up and wait an unimaginable number of times each and every day.

If someone happened to forget or misplace a security card, the consequences were extreme – the possible loss of any identity and access to society because a lost card left a person without a country – homeless and hungry and wandering among the migrant camps on the outskirts of civilization. So, much time and energy was spent making absolutely sure that accident didn't happen.

Security cards kept people in their proper place, blocking access to venues reserved for the upper class. If someone tried accessing a place above their station in society, they were quickly reminded by a flashing red light of where they didn't belong. The embarrassment and constant monitoring was considered a small price to pay for security.

While certain safeguards originated with the best of intentions, the United States had become a victim of paranoia. For the past two decades, the country dedicated an unreasonable amount of time, talent, and resources to running the massive bureaucracy needed to maintain compulsive security measures. This led to very few technological advances being initiated or – more specifically – funded either directly or indirectly by the government. As a result, the hardware still in use remained hopelessly out of date; yet, the best talent was drained for the daily maintenance of legacy systems used to absorb, catalogue, and act upon the overwhelming amount of incoming information. Although voice and facial recognition had been in use in many places for many years instead of physical cards, even a simple change like that had become impossible because of the resources that would have been required to implement the enhancement across thousands of programs and data storage servers.

Public Transportation and the Shrinking World

Public transportation far outnumbered private cars, which had become too expensive for most people. Subways always ran standing room only and highways became the playground of trucks and buses. Improvements to infrastructure, like technology, were nonexistent. Life remained surprisingly unchanged.

As the holiday got underway, you'd expect people to have a livelier step and be quicker to smile as they headed home, but they knew they still had to walk through politically divided neighborhoods. If seen by the opposing factions, they'd be called names and harassed. Pedestrians were sometimes robbed and beaten, so most tried to avoid these neighborhoods or at least get through them as quickly and unobtrusively as possible. Nevertheless, grocery stores were filled this night with people picking up last-minute ingredients for family gatherings that would disintegrate into "Complaining Day" dinner conversations to better reflect the prevailing mood of groups inevitably split by politics.

Even Christmas had become a lightning rod for controversy. Since the holidays tended to disrupt all-important daily routines, some people felt they should be eliminated altogether. However, more and more people began to wonder whether those routines were worth the effort.

The New Year

Once Thanksgiving and Christmas had come and gone, and the calendar was flipped from December 31st to January 1st, the world typically settled back into a mercifully predictable routine.

Up at 6:00 a.m. – breakfast, shower, catch the news, get out the door by 7:45 to pick up a ride and get to work by 8:30. Such was the daily schedule of life for most of the country's residents.

Orderly. Predictable. Reliable. Safe – at least until one ventured into the wrong neighborhood. Basic needs were addressed and desires suppressed. Just as individual cars largely ceased to exist, giving way to various modes of transit for the masses, most people now lived in identical government housing complexes that were long on utilitarianism but short on personalized elements of taste. The days of keeping up with the Jones were long gone.

Strict dress codes at work relieved people of the need to spend large amounts of time and money on wardrobes that would call attention to themselves and set them apart from others less fortunate. About 70% of the people wore uniforms of various shades of grey to work every day.

Over the course of 20 years, society had finally succeeded in creating a world that eliminated much of the unsettling unpredictability of life . . . and much of the vanity that drove people to make bad choices. However, the holidays inevitably brought some of those qualities back to the forefront as buyers tried to get gifts that stood out, rather than blending with the crowd.

Great strides had been made in regularizing life and fulfilling basic needs; so, you'd expect people to be happier and more content. Instead, too many seemed to get absorbed by apathy – leaving blank stares, dragging footsteps, lethargic gaits, and rubbery handshakes – all occurring within a grey landscape populated by identical structures.

Distant memories . . . old folk tales of a way of life that was richer and had more variety and meaning — more freedom and less boredom – persisted and were now the stuff that filled modern legends and gave them life.

DIVIDED STATES

This was the everyday existence for most citizens of the United States until a revolutionary spark lit a fire within an increasingly large faction of the local population.

New Year's Eve

New Year's Eve – the selection of this day was intentional. New beginnings. Fresh starts. A future wide open to possibilities.

The weather was uncharacteristically cooperative with subzero temperatures and a somewhat heavy snowfall – conditions that often-discouraged long-distance travel but in no way affected the ability to move about the immediate vicinity. Basically, a typical January forecast for the northeast corner of the United States.

As David Evans prepared to walk on stage, he could picture the countless Times Square, ball-dropping ceremonies he'd watched on TV over the years. However, this night's celebration would be quite different.

As David took his place among the large group assembled on the platform, the sound of a bugle played taps as the flag was slowly lowered to coincide with the clock approaching midnight. Despite the cold, the entire population of the town was gathered around stage – like a gigantic theater-in-the-round.

As the music stopped, the flag was respectfully folded and placed in a sealed container – soon to be displayed in a glass case at the historical society with other artifacts that were part of the past but no longer had a role in the present or future.

Meanwhile, David delivered the new flag to center stage . . . so this symbol could be raised as the hour struck midnight.

The crowd, which had been somber and remarkably silent, grew raucous and excited as a single trumpeter introduced Penndelom to the world.

Remarks of the First Citizen, speaking into the microphone at center stage, were simple and straightforward:

"Tonight marks the start of our new country. While we thank the United States for many good years as part of that great union, we must now venture off on our own. The time is right. The union is dying and no longer serves the best interests of member states. While the path ahead – going alone – is certain to be fraught with challenges, we no longer have a choice. If we want to preserve our principles and nurture the spirit of individuals, we must do so by ourselves."

At first, the crowd was quiet.

Then, applause began.

Then, a large impromptu parade marched through town.

Although that last part of the festivities was unplanned, people seemed unwilling to disperse and appeared to need the reassuring sense of solidarity.

Penndelom, formerly-of-Pennsylvania, was now a self-declared free state.

Penndelom was a small city with a population of 100,000. While hardly self-sufficient, the community had a history of both agriculture and small manufacturing, which suggested the people stood a chance at becoming autonomous in a fairly short amount of time with the help of a few key trade agreements.

Whether the United States would permit such a departure was another matter. Penndelom could certainly be squashed in short order by a single military action. However, several dozen similar acts of secession had cropped up across the country in recent months, so the government appeared to be in a state of crippled inaction while politicians debated and avoided voting to retaliate against fellow citizens. Meanwhile, the areas that had seceded were adjusting, adapting, and learning the art of survival on their own. Recent rumors suggested several states were voting on secession. If that occurred, the acts of these small communities were likely to be ignored when faced by that bigger concern.

The world was changing, and the number of secessionists sprouting independently in all corners of the country was indicative of a growing dissatisfaction within the crippling bureaucracy of a vast unified government. Bickering among the diverse groups comprising the people was now the dominant voice heard in the U.S.

David Evans – both philosophically and temperamentally – fell into this category of people driving such actions as those taken by Penndelom.

David was never certain exactly how he had ended up on stage on New Year's Eve – playing a very visible role in the ceremony. He was basically a loner – not a joiner – known for his strong sense of independence. He generally steered clear of situations that drew attention to himself.

While these characteristics were actually at the heart of the separatist movement, David was no one's poster boy. Nevertheless, he did believe in the cause and, therefore, did not balk too much about being swept into a more visible role.

"So, David, what comes next?" asked his friend John O'Hara.

"I don't know. I'm not part of the inner circle. I simply ended up on stage because I was nearby and knew how to turn on the lights.

Could as easily have been you. Still, I would imagine that a town meeting will be called to have a quick election. Till then, the Separatist Committee will keep running things on an ad hoc basis."

"Doesn't sound very organized," said John.

"Step 1 – today's events – was all that was on everyone's minds. Thinking about Step 2 seemed like a luxury."

"Well, I'm cold" said John, "and ready to head home for a nice cup of coffee . . . or perhaps something stronger. Care to come?"

"Thanks anyway, but I've had enough intoxicating excitement for one day."

"You do know that picture of you carrying the flag will be splashed across the Internet by morning, right David?

"I suppose so."

"Potentially making you a target for the good ole U.S. to squash."

"Overly dramatic . . . and I don't squash that easily."

Walking home, the hour quite late, David could see very clearly in the harsh stadium lighting that lined both sides of every road – trying somewhat successfully to turn night into day. However, he did not bother absorbing the sights. He didn't really see the clean, modern lines of tall building after building – the smallest probably 10 stories high. The monotonous gray monochrome of the synthetic stone material used to cover the small portion of the structure that was not glass in no way seemed unusual to him. For David had grown up in this town within a landscape that changed little for two dozen years. Square and rectangular boxes with straight geometrical lines created a cold, sterile setting seemingly at odds with nature, which featured a much broader palette and an infinite number of curved shapes that sometimes closed to form circles, ovals, and ellipses.

In other words, the landscape was the perfect setting for a country that – according to secessionists – was now in decline.

The United States no longer resembled the original country envisioned by the founding fathers or even the less dynamic versions of the next few hundred years. The government ruled with an iron fist that resulted in overly organized structures that controlled activity from the national level down. To maintain this kind of rule, an extraordinarily well-developed bureaucracy was required.

Spontaneity was an impulse easily sacrificed to make sure a strong sense of order existed. Instead, efficiency became the watchword of the day. Since every action had to be documented, approved by many, and stored in numerous places, handling of the trillions of transactions became crucial and increasingly impossible. To succeed, life was managed electronically in a paperless world that nevertheless still required legions of middle management types in roles now misnamed "paper pushers" – the heart of the economy.

Every step of every day was catalogued by computers reading ID's scanned before any movement or action. Despite advances in technology, the sheer volume of processing was staggering and starting to implode the system – causing an increasing number of mistakes. While people learned early in life not to lose or misuse their IDs, panic could occur when an optical reader errored and produced a security card failure!

The Morning After

New Year's Day and the phone was ringing yet again. David had ignored the first few calls but was starting to hear cell phone messages arriving every few seconds.

Holiday greetings?

Why was the world so determined to get up early today?

Realizing his chance for continued sleep was gone, David got up but kept ignoring intrusions from outside. Instead, he took a long, slow shower – allowing himself to ease into the day.

Getting dressed, thinking about the previous night and wondering whether his world would really be changing, his imagination just didn't stretch far enough to clearly picture a free state of Penndelom.

Hearing a knocking, he assumed his neighbor must be getting an early visitor, but the sound grew louder as he drew closer to his door.

David lived a very quiet, largely solitary life as an adult. While he certainly had lots of friends, very little family remained . . . so any intrusion upon his daily habits by outside influences was minimal. Although this way of life sometimes made him feel lonely, he was comfortable with himself and his choices.

He certainly hoped to someday be part of a larger family once again. But until then, he was managing just fine with his one sister, her family, and his few very close friends.

"Hello?" he called through the door instead of just assuming someone was outside.

"My name is Jen. I'm from the Daily Herald. I've come to ask you a question. 'What's next?'"

Confused, David said, "I think you're knocking on the wrong door."

"David Evans?"

"Yes."

"One of the leaders of the PRIM – the Penndelom Revolutionary Independence Movement?"

"Hardly. A supporter – maybe. A sympathizer – probably. Beyond that . . . "

"Oh, please! Do you take me for an idiot? You don't get picked to raise the brand-new flag of independence by accident. You've gone viral!"

With that, David opened the door and saw a young woman dressed in jeans, black parka with a fur collar around the hood, and calf-high black boots.

Attractive.

Red-faced from the cold.

"Thank you. Okay to step inside?"

Not too pushy. Seemingly just doing her job.

"Fine. Care to explain? Do I look like your typical revolutionary?"

"What does one of those look like?" she asked, then continued, "I gather you haven't been on the Internet this morning or had time to check the news or social media. Your face is plastered everywhere under some variation of the words: 'Give us liberty.'"

"I never said that or anything else."

"Doesn't matter," she said matter-of-factly.

"I just happened to be the one who was readily available to hand off the flag to the real leaders."

"Doesn't look that way in the pictures," she said and showed him the photo used by her paper that morning.

"Swell. Just swell," David mumbled in dismay as he went to boot up his computer.

"Don't know how to tell you," she said, "but a star's been born. By the way," she continued, "I'm Jen O'Neil."

Well, it turned out Jen O'Neil was right. Everywhere he went on the Internet, he saw himself and the new flag with a headline that suggested his name was synonymous with revolution.

"Step aside Che Guevara," David mumbled to himself.

One particularly inventive publication had superimposed a picture of himself from his high school graduation onto a quote from a classmate that implied he was a budding terrorist in 10th grade – an image reinforced by a college acquaintance who noted that David never fit in; he was always skipping key ceremonies and choosing to stay very clear of the Greek fraternity scene.

Ridiculousness.

Just a matter of time, he thought, before they start collecting comments from his family's priest. Shame his parents were dead; otherwise, they could stake out their house – a thought that made him realize he had better call his sister to warn her and explain the strange photos she'd soon be seeing on her computer.

"So," David said, "I can see you are obviously right, and I appreciate the heads up. However, I really am not a significant part of Penndelom's secession. My appearance onstage was basically an accident. Looking around the apartment, assessing his genuine surprise and overall demeanor, Jen said, "So let's say maybe I believe you. What are you going to do now?"

David looked at her. He sensed that the person, not the reporter, was the part of her asking the question, and he admitted, "I don't know."

Reluctant Hero

Jennifer O'Neil was 25 years old and very new to the newspaper business, but she had an old soul with an outlook on life – and native intelligence – that made up for her inexperience. She grew up in a nearby town and understood Penndelom's recent, crazy posture. She even sympathized and wished her town would take such a foolish action. Nevertheless, she was equally certain the movement had no future and key figures like David Evans would be crushed along with that movement.

David denied the importance of his involvement, but she believed that – while he modestly saw himself as unimportant – she suspected others' opinions were probably more accurate.

She found him interesting.

Trying to decide her next move, she waited for David to make up his mind about the next step he'd be taking. About to prompt him, a video call was coming through on his computer. She heard him say, "Hey, John. What's up? You *never* use this app."

"I wanted to be able to see your reaction. I heard through the grapevine that the Pennsylvania legislature passed the statewide secession declaration, making us one of the first."

"Are you sure?"

"Yep, and I got more. Governor heard about Penndelom and saw a posted social media video of you at the flag raising. You'll be getting a call to participate in PA's ceremony. He saw all those viral 'likes' and smiley faces – and wants in."

"You've lost your mind."

"You remember Peter from 7th grade? Give him a call. He can confirm what I say because he heard it directly from the Governor."

Jen – realizing her good fortune in getting this scoop, waited until the conversation was done and then stated, "Unimportant, huh?"

"Not you, too! He's picked up some small snippet of information and let his imagination run wild. I know him; you don't."

"Mind if I hang around?" Jen asked, sensing an opportunity to see history unfold firsthand.

"What? And watch me eat breakfast?"

"What are we having?" Jen countered as David's cell phone began to ring.

She heard the word "Harrisburg" – the state capitol – and knew John had been right.

"So, who is this . . . David Evans?" asked the governor.

"Judging from the picture today," said his press secretary, "he's one of the leaders of the uprising in Penndelom. The reaction to him on the Internet has been amazing. He went viral almost immediately. Apparently, disgruntled people see him and his actions as a symbol and rallying point of a New World Order, and clearly, they are tired of the old one."

"Should we be worried about reaction from Washington?" the governor suddenly mused aloud – perhaps mentally equating David's notoriety and overnight rise to fame with his own suddenly greater visibility.

"The president is losing power rapidly," said the press secretary. "He's also more than a little bit nuts."

As bad as the situation had become in Pennsylvania, the state of affairs nationally was worse. Originally elected as the Republican savior of the free world, the president's lack of experience and incomplete understanding of world affairs eventually exposed him as a fraud. Domestically, he lacked either the technological expertise to manage the monolithic Washington bureaucracy or the administrative expertise to harness the resources at his disposal to handle technology matters for him. As a result, the system was soon broken, and people began to feel the pain at the local level.

As services stopped being delivered but bills for them – meaning taxes – kept arriving at each level of government, the rebellions began. At first – isolated pockets. Now – throughout large chunks of the country.

Governor Fox of Pennsylvania was the most recent to decide to pull away and set up an autonomous country. The state was large enough and diverse enough with sufficient natural resources to succeed.

"Governor Fox, you've got an incoming call from Washington," announced his assistant.

"Let me talk first," the press secretary suggested, "and do some prescreening. Try to see what they want. Meanwhile, Governor, short of recruiting David Evans to our cause, you need to decide what our official posture on Penndelom is going to be so I can issue a statement."

"So, what did the governor want?" Jen asked.

"Wasn't the governor – just some guy named Carlos Santiago."

"You mean," said Jen, "just the governor's chief of staff and overall right-hand man?"

"If you say so," responded David.

"Sooooo . . . what did they want?"

"Asked me to attend the formal announcement."

"David, that's a big deal. And do what?"

"Nuthin' – just be another face on stage."

"Bull. Don't believe them. At a minimum, you'll be introduced, which will make you appear to be a supporter. And what about Penndelom, which also seceded from Pennsylvania in leaving the United States union?"

"Would remaining part of PA really be such a bad decision?" asked David rhetorically. "I suspect Pennsylvania has a better chance of success than going alone . . . as long as the U.S. doesn't choose to squash us both."

Then, somewhat reflectively he added, "Besides, was the real problem at the state or the national level?"

"Good thought," Jen agreed. "Where did you land in your thinking?"

"I haven't. Anyway, why me? I'm nobody."

"So, you keep saying."

"What was the response? Is Washington going to send troops to Harrisburg to arrest you for treason?" the governor's press secretary queried while looking and sounding genuinely worried.

"He pointed out that we couldn't even keep our own Pennsylvania cities in line – alluding to Penndelom. Until we have proven that we can," he concluded, kind of laughing, "he has a hard time taking our proclamation very seriously."

"Right," the press secretary said. "That's why he immediately called upon hearing the news."

"Still," Fox admitted, "we are going to keep hearing that remark from everybody, which will just distract attention from the seriousness of our cause."

"So?"

"So . . . we need to get Penndelom to rejoin the fold now that they know we share their concerns and are philosophically aligned with them."

"That David Evans could be the key to swinging public opinion our way. Internet stats suggest he is *very* popular – rapidly becoming a key influencer."

Town Meeting

Although Penndelom was a bit too big to have a true, old-fashioned town meeting, they had the technical resources and know-how to successfully set up a virtual gathering that featured the ability to immediately poll the audience for input.

About 10,000, or just 10%, of the citizenry were able to cram inside the large municipal arena used for the rally.

David Evans stood backstage. He had done some A/V work at the facility and was one of the people recruited to help make this meeting happen. Ron Rose – PRIM's leader and a key voice in the secessionist movement – was leading the meeting.

Standing next to David, though not part of the backstage crew, was Jen O'Neil.

January weather in the northeast can usually be relied upon to be rather unfriendly, and this New Year's Day was no exception. The temperature was close to zero degrees Fahrenheit, and light snow had been falling for the past 12 hours, though only about a half foot had accumulated. Nevertheless, these conditions created a clean, white purity across a landscape still lit by holiday lights that gave the snow an iridescent glow.

"On behalf of the new country of Penndelom, I welcome you," said Ron Rose to officially open the meeting. "Today has been quite exciting . . . but now the real work of setting up government must begin. The Separatist Committee of the Penndelom Revolutionary Independence Movement will see that we keep functioning until new leadership is elected.

"The mechanics of voting will be simple. Our Provisional Government will be an 11-member Council – each of them elected by you. The Council will, in turn, select a chairperson. That governing body will be charged with drafting a new constitution. We will keep government very lean with bureaucracy – and *bureaucrats* – kept to a minimum. Tonight," he continued, "we will collect nominations for the 11 Council positions. Since time is critical, and we need to get our government into place, the general election will be tomorrow. All voting will be done by computer – as in the past. No speeches. No promises. No elaborate political platforms of unattainable lies. Just vote based on your prior personal knowledge of the people in question. If you don't recognize 11 worthwhile candidates, vote for the ones you do know and abstain from the rest. We are small enough that such an election process can work, and our methodology will send a powerful message about the type of government we want to become."

"What about Governor Fox's announcement," a heckler shouted from the crowd.

"Doesn't matter," Rose flatly stated, "we're our own country going our own way."

In all, 37 nominees had the minimum number of supporters to be placed on the ballot. The top two vote-getters, by far, were Ron Rose, head of PRIM, and David Evans.

"No thanks."

"I don't really think that's an option in this case," countered Jen. "Especially with the general election being tomorrow."

"You gotta understand," he explained, "even if I were the right personality, I'm not sure we should separate from Pennsylvania now that they've chosen the path to independence, too."

Already getting to know David pretty well despite the short period of their acquaintance, she believed every word, which in her mind probably made him the ideal councilman – he had no personal agenda. "Then, maybe you really *should* seek a council seat to have a voice in government and steer them in Fox's direction."

"Easy for you to say. In a few hours, you'll probably be gone and watching with great amusement from a safe distance."

"Tell you what," she offered, "you take a Council seat, and I'll stick with you . . . stay involved." Secretly pleased to have such an easy way of maintaining contact, she asked, "When's the PA ceremony they want you to attend? Before or after the Penndelom election?" recognizing that the vote better come first.

"*If* I do this, you better be as good as your word!"

He kind of liked the idea of her hanging around.

President King

"Have we heard from Evans yet?"

"He called back and agreed to attend PA's ceremony as long as he had no scheduling conflict – meaning he's not available today or tomorrow but could travel to Harrisburg Thursday or later. However, he did also ask for details about our plans for the free state."

"What did you tell him?" Fox asked.

"The truth. Our plans are a moving target, and we are still trying to figure out the best way of getting a government into place quickly but in some sort of shape we can live with for years and years to come. While we might intend for our interim answer to be replaced fast, we all know those quick fixes can end up having staying power just because a permanent one is hard to find and even harder to get people to agree upon."

"By the way," Fox's Chief of Staff Carlos Santiago mentioned, "David Evans' name is in the Penndelom Council pool by popular acclaim."

"Their version of democracy sounds good in principle . . . but I believe they will find this council of theirs will become unwieldy very quickly."

"And you really think that the best solution is to look all the way back to the original U.S. government when we still had 13 colonies and to try using that as our foundation?" Carlos added, his tone expressing his incredulity.

"Well, yes . . . though don't take that too literally," Fox cautioned. "We want the spirit of the structure and some of the basic tenets. That would be a good start. Besides, that connection will be an easy sell to our fellow Pennsylvanians," he noted as he leaned back in his chair and then asked, "Any word from Washington yet?"

"Fortunately for us, President King has a lot on his hands right now. "California, Arizona, and Nevada have seceded. Guess they're trying to decide whether or not to form a new country together . . .or go forward alone."

"King is such a wild card," Fox mused. "You really never know when he's going to decide to do some crazy retaliation, like building a wall around Pennsylvania to keep everybody out of the rest of the country."

"You're joking, right?"

"Not really," Fox sighed. "People have such short memories."

Hundreds of miles away from Fox's conversation in the northeast, President King sat in his office reading a recent poll about his approval rating in different parts of the country. Knowing that his boss took these scorecards more seriously than almost any other report to cross his desk, his chief of staff patiently waited before hesitantly saying, "Mr. President, I think you better take a closer look at Pennsylvania. Some potentially dangerous events are occurring."

Not responding but slightly turning his head in the direction of the speaker and appearing to listen, the president continued to stare at the report before eventually responding in a quiet voice, "California comes first. Those are the people that voted for me. They are my people. They are the ones that matter . . . and we are seeing signs of unrest among them." Getting more and more agitated as he made this remark, he then growled, "Screw Pennsylvania!" and went back to staring at the results from those parts of the country that had a history of approving of him . . . until recently.

John

John O'Hara was a childhood friend of David Evans. They'd walked to Central Elementary School together every day for six years. In middle school, they'd both fallen desperately in love with Camri Kaminski. In high school, they'd played on the same basketball team that won their local championship before going to the state level . . . and getting humiliated. By college, David had sort of gone into semi-seclusion – a reaction in part to losing both of his parents prematurely. John was one of his few regular contacts with the world at that time . . . though the year before graduation, David very slowly and carefully began to re-emerge from a two-year collegiate cocoon. He formed a relationship with a young woman named Mary, who seemed nice enough – just not all that well suited to David. They cared about very different stuff – never a good sign. When she left, John was afraid David might totally withdraw yet again and was pleased when that did not happen, though he began an extended period in which he lived a quiet, largely solitary routine.

Tonight, as he walked to meet him and that reporter for a drink, John enjoyed the holiday lights . . . the sight and smell of wood smoke coming from several of the chimneys.

John was having a very hard time imagining a world in which Penndelom was a separate country. Though he was an avid supporter of the cause, his imagination failed him . . . and he hoped David might be able to paint a verbal picture of the future that he could clearly see and embrace in a familiar way.

John had sensed an uncharacteristic level of excitement in David's voice, but he wasn't really sure about the source – the new country or the young woman accompanying him tonight.

Initially, John had been amused that David of all people had attained instant celebrity. He actually understood that David was being truthful and more right than not in his assessment of the reason he landed on stage. John also knew his friend quite surprisingly possessed a charismatic leadership quality – so surprising just because of his nature – that seemed to attract the interest of others in him. For example, John knew that if he had been the one, the cameras would not have focused on him, and no video would have gone viral . . . so none of the subsequent events would have happened either.

David, of course, was totally oblivious to this quality in himself.

"So, who is John?" Jen asked.

"I guess you'd say he's my oldest and best friend," he answered . . . while skipping over the details.

David was preoccupied. All of a sudden, he was faced with a variety of decisions, and he knew his actions could conceivably affect more than just himself.

For example, should he become part of the council? On the remote chance he was elected, David felt he should be prepared.

Should he support total Penndelom independence . . . or opt for the seemingly smarter, safer path of remaining part of Pennsylvania?

And . . . should he indeed go to that PA ceremony in a couple of days, knowing his attendance basically announced his support and, therefore, made his decision for him.

Also, who was this woman sitting by his side. Yesterday, he knew nothing about her. Now, she seemed to play an important part in his decisions. Why did her reaction matter so much to him, and could he – should he – trust her?

"So, David," Jen interrupted his thoughts, "have you made any decisions?"

At that moment, John rounded the corner, saw them, and offered his greeting. "I've come to rescue you from a futile night of getting David to talk."

"I'm Jen; new acquaintance and fledgling reporter by day . . . so be careful what you say to me."

"I've officially been put on notice that I'm *on-the-record!*" John joked, while David said, "Can I imagine John opening his mouth at the wrong time, saying the wrong thing to the wrong person? Can I imagine my old friend John doing that? Well . . . does the sun rise in the east and set west? Certain truths can be relied upon!!"

"Thanks, partner. You'll give our new friend Jen the wrong idea."

"What's the word on the street?" David asked seriously, knowing John would have talked to ten different people in the past hour.

"Continued elation over the separation. People haven't begun to process the consequences of that action. As for me, I need a drink. Been a long day."

With that, they sat for the next three hours, sharing stories about growing up in Penndelom and generally becoming better acquainted. Finally, John circled the subject back to current events, wondering, "What's tomorrow's schedule look like?"

"Election results will be tallied, and the members of the 11-person Council will be formally announced at a town meeting at 6:00 pm."

"Do you have your acceptance speech ready?" John asked.

"I have not yet agreed to accept," David countered, "and my election seems like a long shot. People will come to their senses."

'David, you won't have a choice. Once the people have spoken . . ."

Looking in John's direction, Jen said, "Good luck making that point. I tried and failed miserably."

"You really are best equipped for the job," John stated, when Jen added, "I tried that, too. He has a moral obligation to the community."

"On that note, time to go," David announced. "Tomorrow is a busy day. Jen, can I walk you home?"

"If I leave you out of my sight tonight, will I ever get near you again?" she laughed.

"You mean, getting past the Penndelom secret service guards who will be assigned to me," David joked, trying to change the tone of the conversation, and let them know they were being way too serious.

As they each got out their ID card to pay for their drinks and let the system continue to track their movement, David paused to wonder whether the massive government computer and security system still had the ability to register financial transactions and monitor movements – part of the reason the citizens of Penndelom felt oppressed and rallied to take action against the government. Figuring the answer to that question was probably 'yes' unless the rebels had enlisted the help of a computer wiz able to cut the cord, he still felt that little plastic card controlled his life in too many ways to enumerate.

With that, John said goodnight and promised to meet David prior to the town meeting, so David and Jen began walking slowly in the direction of her apartment.

"Believe me," David said to Jen, "I don't take the possibilities of tomorrow lightly . . . but I think people will eventually realize they were just voting for a face that turned up at the center of the action quite by accident. Do I care what happens to Penndelom?" he asked rhetorically. "Of course. We just spent a night sharing stories about a place that is obviously near and dear to us all. And do I know what's right for this town?" he paused again and shrugged, though Jen's continued silence encouraged him to continue, "I know we're better off breaking from the U.S., but that is a no-brainer. That system was irrevocably broken years ago. People were suffering under a bureaucratic government that now existed solely for self-perpetuation."

"What do you picture the perfect solution to be?" Jen asked.

"That's the problem; I don't know. There is at least a part of me that is probably an anarchist or libertarian at heart. If people knew that, do you think they'd still want to vote for me?"

Jen understood that David had picked an extreme statement to make his point, pretty sure that particular quality was not one that defined him.

"That's my building up ahead," she said . . . but was reluctant to have the evening end. "How about coming in for a nightcap?"

Sorely tempted, unsure whether the offer was literal or a euphemism . . . and wanting to believe the latter, David hesitated before answering, "Much as I'd like to do that because this whole evening has been so enjoyable and important in so many ways, I better not. Tomorrow could be crazy, and I better get back in case anyone comes knocking at my door."

"I won't sleep," she said.

"Nor I," he agreed.

"When and how can we connect tomorrow?"

"Don't worry. You can't get rid of me that easily," he said. "I'll come get you tomorrow afternoon. That work?"

"Yes. Don't forget," she said, squeezing his hand. "And don't be late."

The Vote

David tried to sleep but was unsuccessful. He wandered from room to room in his apartment, tried the TV news – which only made the chance of dozing less likely – and finally took a shot of Irish whiskey – Tullamore Dew to be exact. Only then did he manage a couple of hours of rest accompanied by some crazy dreams that had him barreling down a steep hill toward the large black opening of a very large hole. Jen stood to the side and reached out for his hand as he passed by her.

"Can't ask for an image clearer than that," he thought as he took the ritualistic steps to start a new day: coffee-shower-coffee-dressing-coffee-check his phone and e-mail for messages . . . only to find the forces surrounding him since yesterday had not yet begun to subside.

Rebelling against this instant, unwanted notoriety, David tried to stick to his usual routine. However, that proved nearly impossible when his phone showed he had gotten a text message from the governor. Nothing special . . . but a message from the governor – *to him* – no less: "Can we meet before tonight's vote is announced? I'd like a quiet chance to talk."

David chose not to respond.

Checking in with the election committee, Ron Rose asked, "How's the vote going? Any early predictions?"

"The two leading vote-getters are cruising right along," responded Barbara Charles. "Then, we have four people who are way ahead of the rest and likely to be elected. Finally, we have a very close race among about 25 candidates for the remaining five positions."

"So," Ron concluded, "we probably won't have our final list until after 5:00 pm?"

"Sounds about right," Barbara answered.

"Okay. I'll expect to hear from you between 5:30 and 6:00. Doesn't give us much time . . . but we are basically just announcing the council winners."

"No word from David Evans yet?" the governor asked his chief of staff as the two of them and his security escort from the State Police, Matt Stephenson, walked from his office to his nearby residence.

"No, Governor," Carlos Santiago responded, "but the news is full of stories about CA-NV-AZ choosing to form a new community called Southwesterly rather than go forward alone. Everyone is awaiting President King's official response."

"If he uses a strategy against them successfully," Matt Stephenson suggested, "you can bet he'll try the same against us."

Following a moment of silence during which the three of them seemed to consider this remark, Governor Fox finally responded, "Word is he'll be calling in the National Guard."

"At least what's left of them!" Carlos stated. "News reports keep saying he is expected to use force to bring the rebels back into the fold."

"Doesn't he realize that ship has sailed?" Fox asked, expecting no answer. "Or," he continued, "does he know that once they've seceded, he won't get them back and is left with no choice but to try with the shrinking number of soldiers who haven't deserted or returned to their secessionist states." Having said that, the governor thought out loud, "We need to keep Penndelom as part of Pennsylvania. Hopefully, that ship has not also sailed. Losing that community would make us look weak and vulnerable."

"Governor," Carlos said, "I agree and think we must make a statement now to reassure our people that we are strong, not addressing the Penndelom situation directly but having a forward-looking message! Perhaps we even congratulate our sister states of CA-NV-AZ to get newspeople talking about them instead of us."

"Enough for now gentlemen," Fox said as he opened the door to his residence. "To be continued."

David Evans was a student of history. He had enjoyed studying about Medieval knights who took part in Crusades and felt a moral imperative to live a life defending what was right. He also understood that view of the past was highly romanticized – the product of poets and playwrights. In reality, the Medieval period – sometimes referred to as the Middle Ages – was the culmination – and end – of the Dark Ages, which had started back around 500 A.D.

After centuries of a highly unified society and culture under Roman rule, that system of government broke down, and the world gradually became dominated by small feudal communities under local warlords. The land was marred by constant infighting, and a world of lawlessness reduced people to focusing on fundamental needs to ensure survival.

Troubled by the perspective, David saw many parallels between the rise and fall of Rome and the current United States. So, he couldn't help but wonder whether the action of Penndelom was dooming his people – his friends, family, and neighbors – to a modern resurgence of darkness on the horizon.

Trying not to dwell on this particular scary thought, David knew the best antidote to unwanted meditation of this kind was movement – so he was glad he needed to pick up Jen O'Neil before heading to the town hall to hear the election results.

"Those idiots! Who do they think they are dealing with?" President King asked rhetorically, "I've had enough. Let's shut them down!"

"What do you mean?" asked King's Chief of Staff, Bert Bush.

"Let's exile them from our computer system. Blacklist them forever. Eliminate their records and thereby cut all their services and social connections! Those troublemakers will be in chaos in no time and will be begging to come back to us."

"Sir," the chief warned, "You know we've been down this road before. If we go that route, our remaining Techies – which, by the way, do not represent the cream of the crop – tell us we might not have the resources to bring them back online again."

"They're just giving themselves an out in case they fail," King countered.

"Maybe . . . but that's a huge risk to take."

"Not really. I'm right, and I'm tired of pathetic naysayers trying to take away obvious solutions. Our course of action is clear. We've got to stop listening to these traitors."

King's people – recognizing that further argument at the moment would be dangerous – grew quiet until the chief of staff said, "I'll contact the director of our tech staff and ask him to prepare an Implementation Plan — "

"— that needs to be launched this week!" King barked to cut him off.

"Should I also ask our economic advisors to supply an impact statement, projecting the consequences for both them and us when millions of ID's suddenly don't work and those consumers are eliminated from the equation?"

"As long as you don't plan to use that as another excuse for inaction," the President stated but was already turning his attention elsewhere.

"As promised," David said as Jen answered the door.

"I wondered whether you'd try to ditch me," she teased, not really believing that had been a likelihood.

David was curious. He was curious to learn whether or not he'd respond to Jen O'Neil the same way he had the prior day or whether they'd both just been caught up in the excitement of the celebration because he was pretty sure she had felt some of the same feelings as he had.

"I'm just about ready, Councilman-elect. Come on inside."

Entering, David saw a very small rowhouse decorated for comfort . . . a space to retreat from the world and hide in safety.

"Nice nest."

"My one major extravagance. I bought the house a year ago. Got tired of moving and wanted to be able to make changes without asking permission. Bit of a stretch financially, especially at first, but I've been managing pretty well," she concluded and then said, "Let me grab my stuff."

Making eye contact and feeling a familiar rush from the day before, David reassured, "We have plenty of time."

"Have you made up your mind?"

"About what?" he played stupid as he helped her get into her coat.

"I refuse to honor that dumb question with a response. You are not that dense," she then reverted to challenging him to answer her question, "So ...? Well ...?" she asked again.

"We'll see. If I do . . ." he started to respond.

". . . I remember my promise to stick around," she finished the statement.

The town hall was more subdued than the evening before . . . as if people had an opportunity to stop and consider what they had done – a sobering thought.

Ron Rose, David realized, better come prepared to remind them of all the reasons secession was inevitable and necessary.

Heading backstage, David tried not to react to well-wishers, though Jen whispered, "No need to be impolite. They're just happy for you and the town and want to wish you well."

David mumbled something unintelligible and started adjusting the lighting when Ron Rose approached him.

"I'm supposed to get the results in five minutes and hope to start immediately. On my cue, can you bring up the lights?"

"Sure," David replied.

"With newly elected Council members, I don't think we have the luxury of letting everybody speak, but maybe the top two vote-getters should say a few words. The people should hear from more than just me, and I'm told the top two had almost unanimous support with the next group pretty far behind."

Hearing this plan, Jen tried to read David's face – currently set in an impenetrable mask.

"Perhaps just you tonight, Ron," David responded. "Keep the announcement as simple as possible with little or no pomp and circumstance, allowing Barbara Charles, who tabulated the votes, to do her thing – reading off the names in alphabetical order."

Minutes later, Ron Rose stepped to the podium and spoke to the crowd of 10,000 attending the meeting in person as well as others currently watching the proceedings on live TV.

"Yesterday marked a key moment in the history of Penndelom as we announced our independence from a parent that had become overly domineering and unreasonable . . . from a paranoid, claustrophobic system that watched our every step but cared little for our desires." He paused for emphasis before continuing, "Today is equally important as we take the first step in creating a new government and start building the kind of system that will enable each of us and our children, as well as their children, to thrive. Now," he turned and glanced at the woman standing by his side, "Director of Voting, Barbara Charles, will announce the people you have chosen for the Council who will draft our constitution."

"The winners," Barbara said, "in order of the number of votes received are Ronald Rose; David Evans; Miriam Feinstein; Rosemary Chung; Dr. Melvin Konopinski; William Jeffrey; Wilbur Cunningham; Abdul Medura; Penny Nicholas; Madeline Jones; and Mary O'Brien. Congratulations!" she concluded her list. "Will the winners please stand and then head backstage so we can get a picture to commemorate this moment for our historical records and pass along to the media."

As she finished her remarks, David Evans saw a messenger whispering in Ron Rose's ear. He, in turn, nodded and looked momentarily angry before turning to walk back to the podium.

"Thank you, Barbara," Rose said while turning his head to allow his eyes to scan the entire audience. "As you return to your homes tonight, please know that you have our appreciation for taking your participation in our first election seriously, which helped the process be concluded quickly. I'm sure I speak for everyone when I promise that you will be kept fully informed of all progress because we are building a new, traditional democracy," he said and allowed a moment of applause to pass before continuing. As the clapping gradually faded, he announced, "However, I have just been informed that some change of unknown significance has occurred to the online system that we all interact with on a daily basis.

The audience grew suddenly silent.

"What this means, we do not yet know."

Restless movement could be felt as people looked to one another seeking answers to the unspoken question.

"We promise to keep you informed as we learn more," Rose stated. "In the meantime, we ask that you tell us about any issues that arise from this circumstance and document any actions you can no longer do because of this change. In closing, I strongly urge all of you to take this inconvenience in stride."

Slowly, a sense of panic seemed to send a surge of energy through the crowd.

"We knew we'd be dealing with such issues and now get to measure our readiness by seeing just how well we cope."

Rising voices slowly drowned out the last of Rose's remarks, but the reaction slowly subsided to subdued concern seen on the puzzled faces of people clearly uncertain about the way in which they should react.

"Again, I speak for all of our new Council in saying, 'Thank you.'"

Turning to Jen, David said, "Well, I guess I've made my decision – at least part of one."

Governor Fox's face appeared on the television screen below the "Breaking News" banner.

"I'm speaking with you tonight to address two issues. First, I'm sure most of you are aware by now of a problem with your old ID cards. We have been informed by U.S. President King's office that this complication can be considered an immediate response to Pennsylvania's decision to secede. We do not yet know what problems this measure will cause for each of us, though we are dealing with each situation as it arises. While we view this behavior by the U.S. President to be an act of hostility — and we *are* discussing possible responses —

dealing with any impact upon our daily lives is our top priority. Clearly," he paused and then stated, "this impetuous act is another example of the behavior that has made secession necessary." After allowing a moment of silence to pass for emphasis, he moved on to his next subject.

"The second matter I need to discuss is Penndelom. I'm sure everyone is aware that this municipality made an independent decision yesterday to separate from the Commonwealth. We hope the news of our action at the state level will prompt them to reconsider and formally declare themselves to still be part of the new Pennsylvania. They could be of valuable assistance in shaping our new government. I hope to be meeting with the leadership of Penndelom in the upcoming days. While we recognize that separation was necessary and expect the end result to be good, excessive isolationism is a danger we must guard against. I firmly believe that together we will be an even stronger force that will be successful in building a new nation. "I thank you for your support during these difficult times."

"So," Jen asked, "what have you decided?

"I'll do the Council."

'What's your reason? Duty? Obligation? The chance to keep me around a little longer?"

"All of the above and a feeling that events are getting out of hand very quickly and are likely to get worse. Don't know that I can keep that from happening, but I at least recognize the problem!"

"And the ceremony?" Jen asked.

"I'll go. Even though attending makes me appear to cast my lot with Pennsylvania and Governor Fox, not attending also implies a decision and one that could be the key to viewing PA as having weaker support than in reality exists."

"So, where do you think these events are going to land?"

"Wish I knew!" David said.

"Governor Fox," announced Carlos Santiago, "I just tried to access my bank account using my ID – and could not. We're getting lots of reports about people's cards failing. Think of all the different places this piece of plastic was used, and those are the kinds of reports we've been getting. Just to name a few, we've been hearing about building access failures. Credit cards not registering. Social security checks not arriving. Hospital insurance cards not working." Figuring he'd made his point, Fox's Chief of Staff then summarized, "All of these examples had security clearances bundled into the ID. Needless to say," he then understated, "people aren't happy."

"I assume corrective steps are being taken?" Fox asked.

"Our people are making progress, Governor, and expect to have at least a temporary fix by end of day. Fortunately, the software people stayed with us! While the banks seem committed to eliminating *any* government involvement in their systems going forward, getting a new financial platform in place will take time. We don't yet know whether any short-term fixes are available to us."

"Good," Fox said. "By the way, Evans is coming, but told me not to mistakenly confuse his decision to attend as support for PA. At least not yet."

"Doesn't matter," Carlos countered. "People will see him and draw their own conclusions.

Across the continent, the people of CA/AZ/NV were faced with a different kind of urgency. Having made the practical decision to combine their resources and become the independent entity of Southwesterly, some individual hardship was expected, but no one really anticipated U.S. President King sending troops from the Midwest into the area to subdue and arrest all known suspects for treason.

News reports from the region showed footage of this "occupation" while reporters on the air speculated about the authority of soldiers to use force.

Fittingly, the January sky was very gray and threatening on the west coast – a perfect reflection of the people's flagging spirits upon waking.

As planes circled, the naval base at San Diego was put on high alert.

Jen asked David, "Are you following the news from Southwesterly?"

"No. I was busy reading the article you submitted yesterday. Nicely done. Almost seems as though you could have been present behind the scenes," David smiled and joked.

"I'm surprised my editor didn't make more changes," Jen responded. "Definitely reads a bit partisan, though Peter would be sympathetic to the cause."

"I found the speculation at the end rather interesting," David said. "Do you really think King would attack his own people – or rather, people that *were* his own? All of us have kin in that area, so he'd be risking the support of a big piece of his base."

"King never thinks things through that far," Jen countered,

"Are you writing about today's events too?" David asked.

"As long as the paper will let me. Some reason I shouldn't?"

"No reason."

"By the way," Jen cautioned, "the paper tells me ID cards aren't working and starting to create chaos at banking sites. When you have a chance, better try yours and withdraw some cash, assuming you already haven't. I'm hoping we aren't too late!"

The main thoroughfare through Penndelom seemed different. Tall, gray buildings of glass and concrete still lined the treeless street, and the usual amount of human activity could be seen . . . but somehow felt disjointed. Bystanders seemed a bit befuddled and directionless – pacing small circles, scratching heads, looking a bit uncertain about what to do next.

In particular, the small crowd outside a nondescript bank building showed signs of confused agitation – their business inside seemingly concluded but still unwilling to leave the premises.

"Damn," John exclaimed. "Stupid ID card!" His time tight, he nevertheless went into the bank to retrieve his card that had been 'eaten by the machine'."

"Sorry, John. Can't help you," the bank manager said when John approached him to complain. "We've been shut down. When the computer couldn't recognize you, the card got confiscated as an automatic response built into the programming logic of the system to defeat possible fraud. Happened to 20 people already today in just this branch. I'm hearing from other managers that the same is happening at other sites."

"What are you doing about this problem?" John asked.

"Not too much we *can* do. We send a report to our headquarters in Harrisburg who will send a report to the Comptroller of the Currency in Washington – our governing body. Today, no one seems to be answering their phones."

"So . . .," said John, "I'm suddenly nobody. All my records appear to have been deleted – wiped clean, as if I don't exist and never have."

"Unless Fox and the new Pennsylvania government have an answer to give people back their lives, I suspect looting will start soon. People have no money and need to eat."

"Including me," said John.

Finishing her phone conversation, Jen said, "Thanks, Bill. Be careful the next few days."

David, half listening to Jen's side of the conversation, looked quizzically in her direction.

"An old friend who is an officer at the local branch of Northeast Commonwealth Bank. According to him, the news is mostly good. All customer data is backed up and stored in a safe location beyond the reach of the U.S. government, but programs must be written from scratch on a new system that can access the uploaded information. We'll have new separate financial automation, but not for several weeks. People are going to be stuck until then, and minor looting has already started in city grocery markets. Due to various safeguards against fraud, our bankers don't believe the U.S. can *seize* our funds just our access to them, which is huge."

"Makes sense," David said. "I just heard from Ron Rose. He's going to issue a statement advising people who stay inside *not* to lock their doors. Counterintuitive, but those ID cards that are swiped to gain entrance into buildings are all part of a security system tied into the big U.S. government computer. We rely upon individual ID cards to talk to the parent computer to get permission to unlock our doors and allow re-entry. He also said public transportation will provide free rides for the foreseeable future because those systems are tied into the main U.S. computer, too. Shelters are being set up in public buildings, and food banks will be distributing supplies to everyone.

"Pretty ugly situation," said Jen. "I'm thinking King's action was not anticipated."

"In the end," said David, "the cut off will hurt them as much as Penndelom. I'm suspecting that Pennsylvania at large will be better equipped to deal with the blackout."

"PA Military Reserves are being called out to supply services," answered Jen. "I'm sure more resources are available to tide them over while longer-term solutions are found."

"Well," David tried to be a bit upbeat, "during the next few weeks, we will get into the habit of being autonomous and self-reliant. To quote a wise old philosopher: 'That which does not kill us makes us stronger'."

"Friedrich Nietzsche."

Now I know I'm in love! However, instead of voicing this thought, David said, "King is also going to find that he has an increasingly hard time keeping track of what we are doing. That will make him crazy!!"

"So . . . when do you leave for Harrisburg?" Jen asked, "and do you have enough gas since you have no money to buy more right now?"

"Just got a text message from Fox. He's sending a helicopter in about two hours, so we have a chance to meet before the ceremony."

"Wow! A helicopter! A private meeting!"

"I'm going to speak with Ron Rose before going. Get his thoughts on the PA-Penndelom relationship. By the way, you're coming with me, right Jen? I told Fox I'd need a second seat for my guest."

Caught a bit off guard, Jen hesitated.

As much as she liked David – and she couldn't deny she was attracted to him – events seemed to be unfolding a bit too quickly for comfort. On the one hand, she was a journalist, and he was her story – a potentially very interesting one. So, she needed to stay close to him to do her job.

On the other hand, she had a sense – no doubt premature – that this David could become a pretty important part of her personal life, too. That made her more than a little bit nervous but also caused her to want to pursue that path, though perhaps at a somewhat slower and more deliberate pace than current circumstances seemed to allow.

While he was seemingly kind, gentle, and very unassuming, she sensed his life might have a darker side as well, and she didn't know whether she would be willing or able to deal with any baggage other than her own.

He appeared to be a bit of a loner, but she could not tell whether that was from choice or circumstance – though he certainly seemed comfortable with his current lot in life. Did he just not let others into his world? Was he ever involved in a long-term, serious relationship? If so, why, and how, did that end? Could some past event possibly have caused him to go off and live by himself?

She hesitated for a heartbeat, just long enough to have these thoughts enter, then leave, her mind as she looked into his eyes before answering. "I'd love to come but will need to pick up a few things from my place."

Having taken the plunge, Jen had some reservations but no regrets because she somehow sensed that any other response would have pushed him away, and she'd have lost her chance – probably forever – to learn more about him.

"I'll come with you," David offered, "to make sure we can get around. We'll stop at my place, too."

Daily Herald OpED

A Not So Well-Oiled Machine
by Dr. Garfield Payne - Professor
Political Science
Penndelom Community College

The public has been told that the United States government is a well-oiled machine. Reality is starkly different. This article will reveal that reality.

I concede that the government has been successful in delivering services in a timely way.   The people could rest assured of the police patrolling the streets.   The homeless and indigent would be fed at government-run soup kitchens between noon and 2:00 and 5:00 to 7:00 daily.   Medical needs could be addressed at free mobile clinics.   Although tax notices that fund the programs also arrived like clockwork, garbage does get collected and snow removed in a timely fashion.

Clearly, the United States has become a very complicated but well-oiled machine capable of making citizens safe while tending to countless other needs. However, arriving at this juncture has not been easy and has taken years of trial and error – plus political compromise and occasional personal sacrifice – before a level of competency has been achieved that could be considered a success.

After numerous failures, government officials realized that the machine called society could only ever run so smoothly when you kept close tabs on the behavior of individuals and limited their movement and actions to secure the greater good.   This realization gave birth to a security card system that essentially controlled all aspects of the daily lives of every person. It also spawned a group of discontented rebels who felt their privacy had been invaded and their rights as citizens seriously eroded. To them, the cost of human services had become too steep!

This system had survived for quite a while because the population was taught disciplined obedience at a very early age. Schools featured a routine that began with a Pledge of Allegiance and included various rewards for good behavior that made no waves. Even when the bell rang to signal that the school day was done, students slowly marched single file out the door to their waiting buses.

Society had, indeed, become a well-oiled machine . . . until yesterday – when security scanners broke down and government-issued ID cards no longer worked. Now, barely suppressed emotions have surfaced – released by the confusion caused by the system failure. Even as I write this article, many ID-less people are stuck wandering the streets, totally disenfranchised with no clue as to when their access to their own identity might be restored.

Has the time come to re-evaluate the role of government? Or, perhaps we simply need to take a closer look at the actions of Penndelom and their new leaders Ron Rose and David Evans.

The Ceremony

During the two days since the New Year announcement of Penndelom independence, the world had altered dramatically. For food, clothing, and shelter, individuals – with some help from local town officials – had to fend for themselves. Churches had become main gathering points for help with these necessities and to learn the news and latest developments.

People also stopped paying bills. Besides having no money, products and services no longer existed as traditional retail items. When merchandise was needed, bartering provided the only meaningful currency at the moment.

Similarly, communication systems seemed to be down, so word-of-mouth became a staple. Throughout PA, King's decision to revoke access created hardship and extreme enmity for a population from the former states of Pennsylvania, California, Arizona, and Nevada. While sources of power – electricity, phones, water, etc. – still functioned minimally, utilities were no longer reliable.

When David and Jen's helicopter arrived at the pad of the state capitol building, the pilot said, "I'm to take you directly to Governor

Fox. I've got a car ready. Just give me a moment to lock this thing down."

"Sure," David glanced over at Jen, "though the ceremony is not for several more hours."

David's instructions from Ron Rose, and fellow council members, were to listen to any offers but to avoid making any commitments. He could tell that the past few days had undermined their faith in their ability to stand alone, but they wanted to move cautiously and better understand the new shape of PA's government before making any decisions.

Riding in the governor's limousine, Jen and David got an impromptu tour of a town in chaos.

Jen watched as two men smashed a store window. "Did you see that?" she asked David, who leaned forward and asked the driver, "Have you had much looting?"

"Some," the driver said. "But not so much since the PA Reserve soldiers were activated to serve as military police."

They turned a corner as the looters started climbing through the window they had broken, prompting Jen and David to ride in silence for a few moments until the pilot stated, "We're about five minutes from the governor's office. His assistant will be meeting you while I park the car and try to track down some more fuel."

For David, his life had taken on a surreal, out-of-body quality. He couldn't recognize this person who was flying around in a government helicopter enroute to a meeting with a VIP and accompanied by a smart, attractive reporter who seemed to be part of the force that was dragging him into this unfamiliar life … a life spinning out of his control.

So, he felt as though he was hanging on by a thread to some semblance of control as events swept him forward.

He was nervous, disoriented, and troubled — but somehow simultaneously excited. David was keenly aware of the high stakes of the moment and was burdened by the knowledge that a bad decision on his part might affect far more than just himself. It might, in fact, affect the lives of many people. As a result, David moved forward but on a kind of automatic pilot – a familiar feeling he recognized from an incident from when he was a kid. Though many years had passed, he remembered the moment like the experience had just happened yesterday.

He and some friends had been fishing down by the river. The day was warm, so – ignoring past warnings – they decided to go for a swim, though none of them were accustomed to dealing with the current. Once in the water, those who stayed near shore were okay, unlike those who went further . . . and deeper.

Finding themselves swept along by the strong current, he and one of his friends tried to escape the pull of the river but soon grew weary. While he clung to a low branch, the other boy grabbed onto a floating log that was also being carried swiftly downstream. Then, his friend lost his grip and went under.

Not thinking, David released the branch that he was holding onto and grabbed his pal's outstretched arm. He then helped the other boy swim sideways toward shore rather than fighting the current in an attempt to get back to where they started.

Though they kept getting carried further and further downstream, they also very slowly inched closer toward shore until they were able to grab a low-hanging branch and climb onto the embankment.

While the boys ended up several miles downstream, the lesson learned about overcoming difficult challenges and dangerous forces was a valuable one.

Gretchen Moriarty, a key aide to the governor, finished reviewing the day's itinerary. The ceremony was to be followed by a media session and celebratory dinner that would be breaking up at about 10:00 pm. David and Jen would each be given a room at the governor's residence for the night.

"I didn't realize we'd be staying for more than a day. Figured we'd return right after the ceremony."

"That a problem?"

"I guess not," David looked across at Jen to see whether she was okay with that plan, but she just shrugged.

"The governor will see you now. He indicated that Ms. O'Neil is welcome to attend. He is an admirer of her work."

While the capitol building was clearly in a state of chaos, the structure was old enough, and grand enough with a stained-glass dome, to suggest simpler, more affluent times. Pennsylvania had a long and storied history to serve as a foundation for a new nation.

Fox came out of his office to greet them.

"Fred Fox," the governor extended his hand. "May I call you 'David', or do you prefer 'Dave'?"

"Most people use David."

"And you, Ms. O'Neil? Is 'Jennifer' okay?"

"Jen," she responded, already liking the way in which Fox was handling this greeting and the introductions.

"I'm pleased to meet you both, though I wish the circumstances were better. I take no joy in our need to secede from the union."

David and Jen had done their homework on the governor, though he was already pretty well known.

According to the various sources they'd checked, Fox was in his mid-60's. He was a graduate of Brown University with a master's degree in biotechnology from Rensselaer Polytechnic in New York – a prestigious institution in the field. Exceptionally successful professionally and credited with several patents, Fox was a wealthy, self-made businessman who had developed advances in the manufacture of pharmaceuticals. When he decided to run for public office, he put his personal finances into trust to avoid any possible conflict of interest or suggestion of impropriety. The very first time he ran for governor, despite the odds being against him, he beat the incumbent and won the office.

"Have a seat. I'm sure you know why I've invited you to this ceremony – we *need* Penndelom to remain part of PA; losing you is being perceived as a sign of weakness that could prompt King to make dangerous assumptions about our lack of strength and support."

"You get right to the point, don't you," David responded, "which I appreciate. Unfortunately, you got some bad intel from your staff. I'm nobody, and I certainly don't control Penndelom. I've never had nor wanted that kind of influence."

"So, the reason you got an almost unanimous vote into the new town council was . . . what then?"

"An anomaly of false Internet celebrity. My role with the flag was a fluke."

"Maybe yes. Maybe no," Fox countered. "Regardless of the reason, you currently find yourself wielding a lot of power that could be used successfully to help Penndelom actually survive and thrive as part of the state."

"Governor," Jen interjected, "if David knew more about your plans, perhaps he'd feel more persuaded. What will this new nation of yours look like?"

"You mean ours, not yours," Fox corrected with a lopsided smile. "I'm not being evasive when I say — I wish I knew." He sighed, then continued, "We took action against the United States because the relationship had become totally one-sided and intolerable — much like Penndelom's reason for acting. We just knew the alternative couldn't be much worse and would more than likely be a whole lot better." He formed a temple with his fingers. "From the start, we assumed we would need to improvise as we went and respond to the immediate needs of the moment. While that might not be very politically correct, that answer is real." He paused briefly before concluding on a more upbeat note. "However, my goal is to create a constitution that resembles the spirit and intent of the founding fathers. Will that be possible?" Without waiting for anyone else to speak, he answered himself. "I don't know, but that's as close as I currently can come to a plan. We will not let bureaucracy choke us. And we will not let a monster computer security system rule our lives."

"Why all the pomp and circumstance today?" David asked. "With so much that's more important going on."

"I felt people needed some sort of official ceremony to believe the separation was real and to see themselves as part of a new country. Until they hear the news broadcast and see the pictures appearing on social media, the whole concept is too abstract for most people. Nothing over-the-top is planned."

With that, Fox excused himself to answer the phone. Jen looked at David, who seemed lost in thought.

"So, what do you think, David?" Fox asked while momentarily covering the mouthpiece on his phone. "Can I count on you? Not much will be required, but your public support of the position to remain part of Pennsylvania will, I believe, help deliver Penndelom to us." He turned his attention back to the phone for a few seconds. "Well then, find out! I'm not going to be put on hold forever!" He covered the mouthpiece again and picked his conversation back up with David. "I know the question is probably premature based on the landing point of our discussion, but —" His voice suddenly grew louder and more intense as he spoke into the phone, "Are you certain about that? Right. I'll get back to you." He hung up and turned to face David and Jen. "I just got word that King's troops have opened fire on protestors in Southwesterly."

David and Jen looked at each other, completely stunned.

"If you will excuse me," Fox said. "Everything is happening fast these days. I need to let several members of my staff know about the shooting before the ceremony begins in a couple of hours."

"Governor," David started, "I know you have to go, but to answer your question – I can't make promises and don't know what the feelings back in Penndelom will be, especially in light of the president's latest actions. However, I will tell you this – I've personally felt from the start that we might be better off remaining part of the new Pennsylvania, believing that might be our best chance of survival independent of the United States. While I haven't heard anything to shake that belief, I also haven't heard any detail likely to persuade the skeptical."

"Fair enough, David. I guess my best bet is to hope that you will freely share your personal beliefs on public platforms," he said and turned towards Jen. "And how about you, Ms. O'Neil . . . Jen? Have I made any progress with you?"

"I'm a journalist, so I observe and report but don't typically take sides."

"Of course. By the way, our programmers are ready to go live with a new system that will get many of our services back up and running. I'm told they were able to capture and reuse the old ID numbers of PA citizens, which made the task easier. But, no ID cards are required or will be used. I understand banks are working on their own private solutions and more time will be needed to get a financial system in place. However, they are already attacking the problem and a fast solution is in their best interests. I must go now, but let's plan to grab a few moments tomorrow morning before you return to Penndelom."

"Okay," said David. "Just out of curiosity, who will be running the new Independent Nation of Pennsylvania?"

"Like Penndelom," Fox answered, "a special election will be held. I'll be outlining that in my remarks this afternoon. Will I toss my hat into that ring? Probably. I care about this initiative and want independence to succeed."

The ceremony to officially anoint Pennsylvania a free state was held at the large municipal arena in Harrisburg. The former state capitol was soon to become the capitol of the new nation. Although Philadelphia mounted an initiative to try to get Fox to move the government offices, rightfully arguing that its size, resources, and history all suggested that the city would be a more suitable choice, the campaign ultimately failed.

While the capacity of the Harrisburg arena was only about 20,000, the crowd would certainly be large enough to communicate the excitement of the event to the rest of the state watching on their computers and TVs.

Dressed for the occasion, the facility displayed the Keystone State flag with navy and gold balloons and streamers added to create a festive atmosphere. Several high school bands were playing motivational march music and would be playing the PA anthem – surprisingly still very relevant and apropos:

Pennsylvania, Pennsylvania,
Mighty is your name,
Steeped in glory and tradition,
Object of acclaim.
Where brave men fought the foe of freedom,
Tyranny decried,

Til the bell of independence
filled the countryside.

Pennsylvania, Pennsylvania,
May your future be,
filled with honor everlasting
as your history.

Pennsylvania, Pennsylvania,
Blessed by God's own hand,
Birthplace of a mighty nation,
Keystone of the land.
Where first our country's flag unfolded,
Freedom to proclaim,
May the voices of tomorrow
glorify your name.

Pennsylvania, Pennsylvania,
May your future be,
filled with honor everlasting
as your history.

Above the center of the arena floor was a large jumbotron –
reinforced by a full-screen video display behind Fox's podium,
duplicating the image of him speaking at one hundred times the size!
The stage had images of Fox visiting various parts of Pennsylvania.

After David and Jen had finished their conversation with the
governor – a title soon to be defunct – his assistant, Gretchen Moriority,
had taken charge of them for the next several hours. They lingered over
lunch before making their way toward the arena floor with a sound-
and-light check being performed upon their arrival.

"No fireworks," Gretchen said, "because we are indoors, but a laser light show that will make people forget that omission."

As they walked up the center aisle, Gretchen climbed on stage and motioned for David and Jen to follow. Pointing stage-right, she said, "David, that's where you will sit. Jen, you'll be behind the curtain with me."

"No need for me to be onstage," David said. "I'll stand with you."

"Sorry, Governor Fox's orders. However, I understand you will not be asked to make a speech or statement. You'll simply be introduced during his remarks."

"Hey, Gretch," a young man with an intern's badge hollered, "seen the news about out west? Several people killed by National Guard soldiers breaking up a protest. TV commentator made reference to some historical event called Kent State – I'll have to look that up. I didn't know the U.S. ever had a state called Kent."

"Do we know the cause of the violence?" Gretchen wondered.

"Just trying to shut down the protesters. However, everyone seems surprised that the guns had real ammunition. Think they'll be sending troops into Pennsylvania?" the intern asked somewhat nervously.

"Not yet. King is focused on California . . . thank God," Gretchen said before turning to David and Jen. "You two, we have about a half hour until we need to take our places, but I suggest we just stick around until the governor arrives."

"Gretchen," asked Jen, "has Fox made any plans in case King *does* send troops to disrupt the program?"

"Won't happen, but we have drones flying throughout the border area. If any military is spotted, the PA Reserves have been called up and are ready to be mobilized."

About an hour later, the lights slowly dimmed within the arena. A spotlight appeared on Fox as he stepped toward the podium. When the PA anthem finished playing, Fox began his remarks. "Welcome . . . and congratulations. You have taken a very brave step, and history will remember you as founders of this new beginning. I will be brief. While we have much work ahead, we have earned this opportunity to celebrate. That said, I'm sure everyone is wondering – what's next?" He paused a moment to appear as though he was gathering his thoughts. "Obviously, we have to establish a new form of government, and we must do so as quickly as possible because of the many challenges ahead. Our intention is to stay close to the spirit of the original founding fathers. We plan to blend a few national laws with local self-determination, so each community has input into — and control over — the shape of their daily lives. While the underlying philosophy will look back in a broad way, the actual structure of government must better reflect our current society's needs to become as efficient and effective as possible with a minimum of bureaucracy and red tape."

Applause – which had thus far ranged from polite to moderately enthusiastic – suddenly, spontaneously erupted in support of that promise.

"You like the sound of that one, huh?" Fox chuckled. "Our plan is to structure roles similar to those found in business, though each of these officials will be elected. We'll have a CEO — Chairperson/Chief Executive Officer — who will possibly, but not necessarily, be the same person; a CFO — Chief Financial Officer — in charge of economic decisions, currency, etc.; a COO — Chief Operating Officer — who will be a true processing specialist charged with re-engineering key functions and not a euphemism for a Vice President or Lieutenant Governor whose only real job is as a post-assassination fallback; a CRO

— Chief Risk Officer — in charge of the military and national defense; a Chief Technology/Information Officer to rebuild and limit the new computer system created to run our country; and a Corporate Council to oversee judicial operations. Checks and balances will be supplied by a 50-member Board of Directors – some serving the same role as today's legislative branch but in a more streamlined way. These elected officials will appoint the people who work with them."

More applause . . . mixed with conversation among the audience. Fox waited a moment before he resumed speaking, shifting his remarks toward his finishing statement. "While this general outline of a simpler structure is a start, many challenges lie ahead for these officials, and *all* citizens of Pennsylvania. Elections will be held in one month, with winners chosen by popular vote —which eliminates the electoral college. Until then, the current state government will continue to run our new country while also transitioning themselves personally. In closing, I have lots of people to thank," he said and then used some special effects to grab their attention. The band started playing soft background music while video cameras pointed at the individuals mentioned – flashing large 50-foot-high pictures onto the screen on stage behind the podium. Fox ran through his list of about a dozen and a half people, including his assistant, Gretchen Moriority, who stepped from behind the curtain. He then concluded, "Finally, I'd like to introduce one more individual whose role requires no explanation – Mr. David Evans of Penndelom."

Having seen his face reported on the news and across the Internet daily, the audience clapped enthusiastically and slipped seamlessly into cheering at the start of the laser light show.

The performance lasted about 20 minutes accompanied by the orchestra playing music designed to rally and excite the audience. As the light show came to a close, Fox stepped off stage, the arena lights slowly brightened, and the lieutenant governor thanked everyone, reminding them that they should watch the news for further instructions."

The arena was probably about two-thirds empty when pandemonium erupted outside. Several low-flying planes – clearly part of the U.S. Air Force – circled lower and lower with the sound of their engines deafening.

"We're under attack!" someone shouted.

"We're all gonna die!" a woman screamed, with more and more screams and shouting adding to her own, causing individual words to be indecipherable.

David – still on stage at the start of the confusion – quickly found Jen and Gretchen. "I'm going to try to see what's really going on. You wait right here. I'll be back."

Making his way outside with great difficulty, he moved to the top of a long, long staircase and saw a scene of utter confusion – people pushing and shoving, some being trampled by the mob.

Six large spotlights – the kind used to light up the sky to promote a sale – had been set up to shine upon the capitol building and direct people to the celebration. While the planes were, no doubt, relying upon instruments, David figured that turning out these lights couldn't hurt. Thus far, only the equivalent of tear gas appeared to have been sprayed, though the planes now were circling for another pass.

David managed to pull the plug on two of the spotlights . . . and others in the crowd must have liked the idea and endorsed his action by shutting down four others.

The dimming of the lights *did* produce one unintended and surprising effect – the crowd grew silent, only coughing and crying seeming to break the silence.

"They're coming back!"

"Don't worry," David tried to say, but could not make himself heard.   Then, someone handed him a wireless microphone, so he repeated, "Don't worry. If they were going to drop bombs, they'd have done so already and not started with just tear gas,"

While these words seemed to help the crowd become calmer, the first of the planes released its payload – as thousands of pieces of paper dropped from the sky.

"Leaflets!" David said into the microphone.   "They're sending us leaflets. So now we know the good old U.S. has gotten our message and is afraid of what we might accomplish. Guess they can see more and more states taking similar actions – one after another. President King must be worried we'll succeed; you should be proud."

With that, sirens wailed, and emergency teams began to gather up the people who'd been trampled by the crowd.   David and others helped the EMT's perform triage and transport hundreds of people. While few injuries seemed significant, David suspected mass PTSD would be a problem for years to come.

As David tended to the fallen, Jen and Gretchen made their way to his side.

"That was quite a performance," Jen said.

"What do you mean?" David asked while tying a sling for a gentleman with a dislocated shoulder.

Rather than giving him a straight answer, Gretchen said, "I'm sure the governor will want to thank you. Your actions calmed the crowd, which spared others from being hurt like this man," she nodded to the person having his wound bandaged. "How did you know that would work?"

"All I did was turn out some lights – just like other people. Probably part of me thought we'd be less of a target, though that's utter nonsense in this age of advanced tracking and targeting systems. Guess that would mean I did the right thing for the wrong reason. Still, we tend to be led by our instincts --"

"--and yours are obviously good," Gretchen finished his statement.

"Plus," Jen added, "you sent the right message when handed the microphone."

"Say, where *did* that come from?" David asked.

"One of the TV station's sound equipment," Jen answered. "They were on site covering the ceremony and must have recognized that your words needed to be heard."

"The TV crew got the whole 'attack' and our response on camera, so the news will have excellent coverage. Looks like your face is going to be plastered across the Internet yet again!" Jen warned. "Guess I better try to interview you now before the competition finds you," she teased.

With that, the three of them continued their efforts for the next hour till the crowd finally thinned and the smoke cleared.

Governor Fox, in the company of a handful of state troopers, came up behind them and said, "Found you! We've been searching for the past hour. Are you three okay?"

"Never better," Jen joked, looking out at the littered remains of the evening.

"Thank you, all," he said, "for everything," putting special emphasis on the last word. "I'm sure you folks are exhausted, so we can talk tomorrow. For now, I've asked these gentlemen to escort you to your room just in case."

"Sounds good," Gretchen offered as the others agreed, "but, mind if I borrow these guys to help gather up some papers first? I don't want anything sensitive left hanging around in the arena. We can come back for Jen and David in about a half hour if that's okay."

"Okay by us," Jen said, glancing at David for confirmation. She then looked down and asked, "Hey, has anyone bothered to read the leaflets?"

They all just looked at one another, so she picked one up and read it aloud.

GOOD PEOPLE OF THE STATE OF PENNSYLVANIA.

YOUR GOVERNOR AND HIS CABINET HAVE BETRAYED YOU.

THEY HAVE SECEDED FROM THE UNITED STATES,
BUT WE KNOW YOU DO NOT WANT THIS SEPARATION TO HAPPEN.

OVERTHROW THEM AND COME BACK TO US.

ALL WILL BE FORGIVEN!

Meanwhile, someone was playing a local news video clip:

Thursday, January 6th – This is David Robinson reporting from Harrisburg. A night of celebration designed to formally announce the new Independent Nation of Pennsylvania, took an unexpected and potentially tragic turn as U.S. President King retaliated against the separatists. Although the measures used were less harsh than those tried in Southwesterly, they were still sufficiently aggressive and dangerous to cause numerous injuries. The outcome of the night could have been far worse, if not for the quick thinking of local celebrity, and budding politician, David Evans of Penndelom. In the middle of the chaos, he managed to shut down the lights to get everyone's attention and talk the crowd down from their panic.

Hearing this description of both him and his actions, David moaned and grimaced, causing Grethen to laugh and Jen to elbow him in the ribs as the clip continued . . .

As most of you know, Evans came to prominence as part of the group leading the Penndelom secession initiative. He was then one of the largest vote-getters elected to the new Council assigned the task of mapping out Penndelom's future. Seems like the question on the minds of many is:

'What was he doing in Harrisburg?'

Daily Herald OpED

Metamorphosis - A Follow-up
by Dr. Garfield Payne – Professor
Political Science
Penndelom Community College

I am writing this editorial as a follow-up to my earlier piece, "A Not So Well-Oiled Machine." At that time, we had just begun to experience the earliest impact of the government's decision to cut off personal ID cards, which left all of society in a panic and people with no access to their resources. At that time, a world that had been the epitome of predictability was suddenly broken. A few days later, we already have a clearer picture of the impact this decision will have.

Traffic lights are either dark or continuously blink red, bringing traffic to a slow crawl. Streetlights remain out as do the lights of all the stores up and down the main street of town. Surprisingly and to our credit, looting has not become a problem . . . yet. Although people are hungry and increasingly scared, such behavior is alien to a basically obedient population. Despite the fact that the reassuring necessities of life have been withheld by a force they don't recognize or understand, they still haven't experienced sufficient desperation to act out of character.

Individual homes are now dark, too. At 10:00 each evening, neighborhoods that usually cast a warm, comforting glow from the windows of practically every house go dark — in unison, as if someone flipped a giant switch — as people obeyed convention and some sort of unseen inner clock that insisted they were ready for bed. In a world where much of the decision making had been taken out of the hands of individuals by a universal routine that people were *taught to obey or risk being socially ostracized, the sudden loss of a detailed blueprint for living daily life has become disorienting.*

The fact that rules tend to be followed – and followed somewhat obsessively – doesn't mean that people are content. A barely controlled anger – likely borne of frustration – has been simmering slightly below this orderly surface, waiting for an opportunity to appear and ultimately escape to support secession and revolution.

While an objective observer might expect any new-found freedom that shook up routines to be welcome, most folks have become quite disoriented by the sudden loss of rules for living their lives and find themselves asking questions like "How do I know the right time to go to bed, the food to eat for breakfast, or the shows to watch on the television?" The list goes on and on. While individuals have always been free to ignore such conventions — no alarms went off, no one was arrested, etc. for failure to stay with the herd — everyone grew up with a need for peer acceptance. Experience taught people to want to avoid being the only red house on a block in which all others are white. However, I close this article by challenging everyone to consider buying some red paint!

Jen

Jen O'Neil grew up as the second of three daughters in a small town next to Penndelom. Her father was an elementary school teacher and her mother was a feature story writer for the local newspaper. Both retired about five years ago and were alive and well.

Her older sister, Olivia, was always the family star – a straight-A student, popular, and musically gifted. Her younger sister, Samatha, was developing into a rebel – one without a cause. Jen was the classic middle child, sandwiched between one sister who had life handed to her and one who was a high-maintenance college sophomore who figured out the best way to get her share of the attention was to major in drama – for which she clearly had a natural talent!

Though Jen was not the type to be elected class president or prom queen — two titles that belonged to her older sister — she was nevertheless quite successful and popular herself. She was a good student in high school who became an excellent student in college. It was an improvement she attributed to finding a better academic niche for herself. She had started out as a political science major – which she viewed as prelaw – but soon became disenchanted. The professors were uninspiring, and her classmates were superficial – focusing on a very narrow and conventional view of 'Poly Sci' as synonymous with two-party politics rather than engaging in meaningful exploration of the underlying structure of society and all that had gone wrong.

By the second year of college, she had switched her major to communications with a focus in journalism. This change was not a perfect match to her personality but was definitely a better fit and was one that gave her the opportunity to use her writing skills – an activity she enjoyed and viewed as recreational.

Although her older sister liked to remind her that *she* graduated magna cum laude, Jen was pleased to have graduated with regular honors. She was even happier when she got a full-time, entry-level position at the local newspaper right after graduation. Low person on the totem pole, most of her assignments ranged from the unimportant to the even less important, and much less interesting, until she got lucky a couple of months ago and did a story on Governor Fox's newest educational initiative.

The feedback she got from government workers in Harrisburg and her peers was good, and Fox liked her work, so she was given access to information and people to do the rest of what became a series.

This connection to Fox got her assigned to the Penndelom secession story, which caught her imagination and interested her. Although she had already turned in her article on the event, she'd followed a hunch and decided to go knock on David Evans' door.

She had expected him to be an outspoken revolutionary or a misanthropic pseudointellectual. What she found was a smart, unassuming man with a strong dislike for being in the spotlight. She wanted to get to know him better and – so far – her initial encounter had left her wanting more. However, she was also very wary of allowing herself to get too involved too fast – partly because he was part of a story she was covering and partly because he still seemed to her to be a huge unknown who didn't let people into his life very fast – at least she'd heard that was his reputation.

If that really was the case, she wondered whether he was unwilling to form close relationships . . . or unable? Having run into both types over the years, she knew the next question was *why*? Did he scare people away . . . or was he really just a shy introvert caught up in the world of politics, which tends to attract very extroverted people.

While Jen did not sense any sinister quality in David, she had learned to be careful. Was he truly an unwilling participant in his recent rocket to political fame, or was his reluctance just a self-serving act?

Jen always had a pretty strong sense of who she was – what she liked and what she didn't. She tended to have a small group of very close friends, rather than a large group of somewhat familiar acquaintances, which she always thought was the case with her older sister Olivia.

While her inner circle included some boys, she'd only had that elusive thing called a 'boyfriend' for a grand total of about three months at the end of her senior year in college. And, that relationship was less than satisfying. After a few attempts at sex, she decided they had no long-term future and broke up with him. In retrospect, she realized their chemistry had always been off, and she was convinced he'd played at being devastated far more than reality warranted.

These days, she suspected she was at a crossroads – not necessarily unhappy but not particularly fulfilled by her professional or personal life. Although she certainly never considered herself a political radical, she did have a very strong awareness of the world gone awry – a sense of disillusionment that had grown over the past five years. Perhaps that's the reason the Penndelom story piqued her interest.

On the night of the PA ceremony, Jen felt she'd seen a different side of David emerge, one that featured a willingness to act decisively and alone when the situation – and his personal convictions – warranted. Plus, he did so with humility while trying to preserve his anonymity.

After hours of dealing with one immediate need after another, the scene had finally grown quiet, and Jen and David sat alone on the steps of the arena.

"Quite a night," he understated.

"Can't say I ever saw any of that coming," Jen responded. "So, you still think Penndelom would be better off sticking with PA? As is, the town might fly under the radar of the U.S."

"Only for a while," he glanced at his watch and then asked, "You hungry, Jen?"

"As a matter of fact —" she stopped speaking when she saw the governor's aide approaching.

"Hey, Gretchen," they said upon her arrival. "Everybody okay?"

"I'm fine as is the governor and the rest of his staff. Needless to say, tonight's dramatic conclusion was a warning. King wanted to show us just how easily he could squash our rebellion. Those leaflets could have just as easily been bombs."

"I assume," David responded, "that Governor Fox was not overly intimidated."

"No. In fact, he sent King back a leaflet with a handwritten message inviting King and the now-somewhat-smaller-United States to become part of the new Independent Nation of Pennsylvania."

"Good for him; I like his style!" David exclaimed as Jen took notes.

"That on the record, Gretch?" Jen asked.

"You bet. Why not? Feel free to add that to your story."

"The governor is looking forward to your meeting tomorrow morning. He asked me to get you something to eat and to show you to your room at the mansion."

Jen had no regrets about deciding to accompany David, but did feel rather vulnerable as she realized she was suddenly dependent upon this near stranger for transportation, food, and lodging – pretty much everything – in this ID-less world they'd now entered.

While for some unknown reason she trusted David, she also knew that people seldom had full control over the outcomes of the hands they were dealt. That said, his presence still seemed to instill a sense of energy in her. It was almost enough to make her forget that she'd only known him a couple of days under the most unusual of circumstances.

While she sincerely hoped that David reciprocated her interest, she could feel her insecurities rising to the surface. Living in the shadow of a sister who excelled in so many ways – looks, intelligence, personality – Jen felt like she never quite measured up. Her nose was too big, her breasts were too small, and her skin was too pale. She also felt more than just her appearance was lacking; she did not believe she was sufficiently creative to have a truly first-class mind. When she compared herself to someone like Gretchen Moriarty, she felt a wave of inferiority — and jealousy.

She knew she was being ridiculous, but it was further evidence of the depth of Jen's attraction to David.

So, while she accepted David's invitation and found herself aboard a helicopter bound for a meeting with the governor, she kept questioning her judgement – wondering whether she would measure up to whatever the future might hold.

"I suppose we should have asked for two rooms," said David, looking about the place after Gretchen said goodnight and closed the door behind her.

Mustering her courage, Jen smiled and said, "No need," as she nervously took David's hand.

"I should warn you," he said, gently running a finger along her jaw, "I've been told I talk in my sleep." His touch made her skin tingle, and she felt her reservations and inhibitions starting to melt. That was when the phone rang, and someone came pounding on their door. They remained motionless a moment longer – trying to force the clock to stop. However, the knocking didn't — and the moment was lost.

Perhaps she was just caught up in the excitement of the evening or was drawn to this new side of David she'd witnessed earlier, but she suddenly felt quite certain he was worth getting to know better — intellectually as well as intimately. Besides, she had instinctively liked him from the start and greatly disliked dealing with regrets over a missed opportunity.

"What's up?" David asked as he opened the door enough to see a rather young-looking state trooper with an exceptionally serious face.

"Radar picked up more planes. We don't know whether we are looking at more leaflets or have had our warning and are now about to be punished. So, the governor wants everyone down to the lower level."

"Okay. Thanks," David said as he started to close the door."

"Sorry, Sir, but we are supposed to wait and escort you."

Jen stepped out into the hallway just as Gretchen popped her head out two doors up.

"Wait for me," she said. "I don't want to have to be alone with this Harrisburg crowd."

"Sure," Jen answered, though the trooper did not look pleased.

"Crummy timing for an air raid drill," was about all David could bring himself to say as he took one last look at that large inviting bed and closed the door behind them.

"Hopefully won't last very long," Jen said, "so we can all get back to what we were doing."

"No way of knowing, Ma'am," the trooper responded.

Despite the interruption and the uncertainty of the mission of the planes heading in their direction, Jen felt more positive than she had in a very long time. In fact, the prospect of change was inviting.

Though the life she had known was now more than likely gone, she felt hopeful about the future and about getting a fresh start in this new country. Whether her world ended up being just in her own Penndelom-like town or as part of a separate Pennsylvania, she relished the idea of being simpler, smaller, and perhaps finally free from the ever-watchful eye of a national security system that knew and watched her every move. She expected some hardship. On their trip to the Governor's mansion, she was already seeing signs of a world in which the financial structure had collapsed and knew the situation would just get worse. For every homeless person, five more would soon be added to their ranks, making the food and shelter lines grow longer – and people shorter tempered – but she felt confident they'd adjust.

Once they got settled in the basement safe-room, and with this uncharacteristically positive outlook, Jen pulled out her laptop and quickly drafted her story for the paper. She had no time to dwell on the details but needed to get the article out – so she stuck strictly to the facts, believing she'd have more opportunities to explore the meaning of the night's events in her follow-up pieces. Typing "The End," she finished her electronic submission to the paper but was sure to include a note that promised another feature for tomorrow.

Sensing David's presence behind her, she could easily picture him being part of that new life she imagined earlier, and she wondered whether he was experiencing any of the same thoughts.

From his vantage point, David felt as though too much had happened too quickly to digest or understand, and he just wanted time – and the world – to stop long enough to get his bearings. He felt his life was no longer his own, and he dreaded making a misstep.

From the moment he showed up at that event New Year's Eve, his small corner of the universe had become a place he barely recognized, and he found himself living moment to moment – trying his best to navigate his way through immediate events that had taken him into uncharted territory.

And, he wondered, who was this Jen O'Neil who had suddenly become such an ever-present – and increasingly important – part of his existence. He knew she was smart, attractive, very much alive, *and* her entry into his life coincided with all sorts of surreal events.

If someone had told him that he'd be involved in – and become a poster child for – revolution, be pushed into assuming an elected position, be flying around the state in an official helicopter, and be about to meet the governor, he'd have laughed at the ridiculousness of the scenario. Such experiences were antithetical to his personality and yet had become his reality.

So, what *did* he know among all the new unknowables?

He knew he had to keep going moment to moment, because he couldn't imagine another way of surviving the current maelstrom.

He knew he was *not* the person being portrayed to the public and didn't have a clue who the hell that guy was!

He knew he had no choice but to try to do as little damage as possible with any mistakes he might make along the way.

He also knew he wanted his old obscurity back.

Perhaps most importantly, he knew that he wanted to keep Jen O'Neil in his life and was very much afraid she'd be gone as soon as she realized who he really was, finished her story, and/or recognized her actions as madness.

David did recognize that Jen was at least partly responsible for leading him back into greater involvement with the world. She attracted – and was a catalyst for – change.

Meanwhile, time and the tides of events continued to sweep David toward an uncomfortable future.

As much as he liked some of the new elements of society and as much as he sympathized with the political posture of the new world, choice – and the exercise of free will – no longer felt as though they were options available to him.

Announcement by David

Sacramento.

Absolute chaos.

As the first bombs hit, the people panicked – some crowding into the nearest building while others poured out of the structure next door. Clearly, no one knew the right response, though *everyone* felt fear.

Pushing.

Shoving.

People falling on sidewalks and in the middle of the street.

Sirens blaring.

Children crying.

Approximately six bombs had been dropped in a very congested area.

Phones and digital watches began issuing blaring warnings, while somewhere a radio announced a special report:

"Breaking news!! The three-state western rebellion continues. President King announced that a bombing raid is now underway, but he noted that measures were being taken to minimize the loss of life."

Experiencing technical difficulties, emergency services were very slow to respond. The removal of the three Southwesterly states from the U.S. computer system had essentially disabled the EMT's from that area, and people were dying while waiting for help. Panic attacks, heart attacks, strokes, and other stress-related illnesses were taking their toll.

"The President of the United States did this to us!" was cried by many in utter disbelief.

Meanwhile, back east in Penndelom, Ron Rose met with nine of the other duly elected council members. After expressing his condolences over the atrocity occurring out west, he noted, "David did us proud last night. Between his actions and Fox's remarks, Penndelom will be center stage in the national news with David again dominating the Internet!

That said, Rose moved onto the first piece of business for the council – the reason for this very quick, emergency meeting.

"We've all heard Governor Fox's remarks and his offer to Penndelom. Do we want to keep moving forward alone, or do we accept his offer to remain part of the new Independent Nation of Pennsylvania?"

As the members of the council weighed the pros and cons, several people with the most extreme views were nearly shouting, "Why get rid of one master just to immediately wear the shackles of another? Admittedly, Fox is not King, but he'll still be our boss."

"Fox is a good guy, and I trust him," a more moderate member countered. "We'd stand a better chance of survival as part of PA."

"Maybe we should have just stuck with the United States and not separated at all."

As several people around the table nodded in agreement, a low-flying plane passed overhead, and the sound of several bombs exploding could be heard.

"*That* help anyone make a decision?" Rose asked. "Bear in mind, those were likely just a warning – not a full-fledged attack."

That said, he immediately took another vote. The council remained unanimous in their continued support of the Penndelom's separation from the U.S. but was deadlocked five to five in their vote to rejoin Pennsylvania or keep Penndelom separate from everyone.

In Harrisburg, the scene was virtually identical to that played out in Penndelom. Several bombs had been dropped. Given the panic and confusion of the previous evening's flyer run, the people took the current attack in stride.

Confined to the Governor's bomb shelter, David and Jen were resigned to spending the rest of the night underground. Although David remained wide awake and alert, Jen was fast asleep – her head on his shoulder.

As they sat, he heard a nearby voice whisper, "That's him!"

"Are you sure?"

"He's the one I saw on the T.V. last night and the Internet this morning."

The space they were currently occupying had been constructed many decades ago during that period in U.S. history known as the "Cold War." Use of the term "bomb shelter" to describe the basement room of the Governor's Mansion was being generous: four walls with no windows plus a floor and ceiling – all made of concrete. While some of the structural details had been updated, except for the addition of Internet access, the amenities had not.

Tonight, about 50 people – including the governor, his family, some immediate staff, and his secret service/state trooper bodyguards – were crowded into a space designed for half as many bodies. Fortunately, everyone was on his or her best behavior.

Sitting between Jen—whose head was still resting on his shoulder – and Gretchen, David settled in for what promised to be a long night ahead.

"Seems like she can sleep through anything – I'm jealous," Gretchen said.

"Long day with lots of travel at the end."

"David, do you think Penndelom will ultimately stay with PA?"

"Hard to predict, though I think some people have already begun to suspect that going alone might doom us to failure."

"You going to try to help that process?" she asked. "You're a celebrity, a hero — again, after last night — so a statement from you could be a difference maker," she concluded just as another group of planes could be heard flying overhead and dropping more bombs.

They waited out the rest of the night in the shelter with Jen only rousing long enough to ask, "Were we just attacked again, or was I dreaming?"

Come morning, the door opened, and the head of security said, "The area is now safe, so you can go back to your rooms."

The Governor, moving through the crowd in a practiced, skillful way, said to David, "Just wanted to remind you that we are getting together in about 15 minutes."

Upon exiting the shelter and returning to the upper level with windows, David could see the damage done to the immediate area.

He and Jen returned to their room and had just enough time to freshen up before meeting with the Governor.

"Did you get enough sleep?" David asked.

"I felt like I was frustrated and struggling in my weird dreams," Jen responded, "so less rested than the amount of sleep might suggest. What about you? Did you sleep at all?"

"A little. I don't require much."

"How about Gretchen?" she inquired carefully. "She get any sleep at all, or did the two of you just visit?"

"She was awake and was rather envious of your sleep!" he joked.

They joined Fox as he finished getting his briefing on the damage done by the bombing raids.

"Bad enough," the governor concluded, "but could have been worse. David, I see you and Jen survived the long night."

"Yes. We're fine," he responded as she nodded her agreement.

"Good." He sighed and looked at the papers on his desk before continuing, "While Pennsylvania is in no position to retaliate and launch a counter-offensive, I believe our convictions have been strengthened. Some of our computer functions will be restored soon, hopefully accompanied by a renewed sense of confidence. Our banking partners promise we will have separate financial data online this week and that basic processes will be restored. King's attempt to cut us off," he concluded, "will actually make us stronger and more self-sufficient even faster."

David looked at Jen to watch for her reaction as he asked the governor, "Any chance I could get your press secretary and a photographer to join us? I'm ready to make a statement for release to the media."

"How about TV?" the governor immediately asked.

"You're well trained by your PR staff," David joked, "but – no thanks. The Internet, newspapers, and social media will do fine."

"Don't you want to secure a job in the new government before you spend your collateral?" the governor said, half-jokingly. "Right now, you hold all the cards."

"Not interested but give Ron Rose an important role. He's your man!"

The Governor waved as David and Jen boarded the helicopter. As soon as they took off, a member of the crew said, "Mr. Evans – "

" – David."

"I just received a draft of your press statement with instructions to read the piece to you for approval."

Dateline – Harrisburg, PA

Amid the recovery from the bombing of Harrisburg occurring last night, newly elected Penndelom Councilman David Evans offered the following statement:

"While I fully sympathize with all the reasons Penndelom seceded from the U.S., I believe we should now recommit to remaining part of Pennsylvania, which has also separated from the United States. We are philosophically aligned, and we each have a better chance of surviving, and eventually prospering, by joining together. I feel confident that the citizens of Penndelom

will be allowed to participate in the upcoming PA election and will have a chance to be represented with a voice in the new government.

Thank you for your attention to this all-important matter. Whatever is ultimately decided, the people of Penndelom will have my support."

The scene from the helicopter above was deceptively peaceful. The sun was shining, and the white snow below had a look of purity and simplicity that belied the havoc of just hours ago.

"Did I do okay?" David asked Jen.

"Yes. Simple. Honest. Straight to the point," she answered. "I'd expect no less, and I thank you for the scoop," she teased. "I just e-mailed my story and your statement to the paper."

"Happy to oblige."

"Where to in Penndelom?" the pilot asked.

"Any open field near the center of town."

"Seriously, David, do you think Ron Rose and the Council will be mad that you acted independently and didn't give them a chance to weigh in first?"

"After a night of bombing on the east and west coast? If they can't understand that change of circumstances, we got even bigger problems."

Looking Backward

Looking backward with perfect hindsight, the year was the beginning of a season of upheaval, and a period of transition was clearly underway. As the United States began to break apart, the once iron-fisted control of the central government over all aspects of life began to loosen. This glimpse back illustrates some of the shifts that were occurring.

A Time of Change

The world was in a state of flux with an odd juxtaposition of high tech and low/no tech suddenly side by side – either a foreshadowing of future life or perhaps a temporary dislocation brought about by revolution and political conflict.

Computers, communications equipment, and weapons of war still existed and were in everyday use, but individuals could no longer find new programming on TV, except for 24-hour news.

Everyone had appliances to make life easier – until these conveniences broke down with no one left to fix them and no replacements anywhere to be found. Supplying the military was the focus of all efforts involving the transport and distribution of goods during these uncertain times.

Schools continued to operate, though single-grade classrooms were now in the past due to a shortage of teachers reporting for work. While mixed-grade classes seemed to suffice for the short-term, people who valued education expected long-term inadequacies to be suffered over time.

Food was becoming just a matter of back-to-basics necessity with menus getting shorter and simpler to match the shrinking availability of ingredients and talented/experienced cooking help.

Medical care suffered, too. Overworked Emergency Room staff now provided 90% of all treatment with most major procedures being delayed until hospitals fully reopened – which was clearly an ineffectual band aid, especially for the elderly and those fighting chronic or major ailments.

Religion witnessed two extremes with some people opting to worship remotely via radio or unstable Internet connections, while others gathered in spontaneous, grassroots revival groups that relied upon prayer to release emotions and combat the fears threatening to overwhelm them.

Due to shortages in almost every category of life, large extended families became the norm as near and distant relatives gathered under one roof to share resources and expenses – two keys to better safety and personal security.

Dealing with the daily necessities of life left little room to reflect upon the past or speculate about the future; such thoughts were becoming a frivolous luxury with the disintegration of society occurring quickly. Furthermore, this process was happening across weeks, not months, prompted by the threat of civil war and internal conflict. However, the stage had been set years in advance as systems deteriorated and were poised to collapse due to ongoing neglect plus the absence of back-up systems. Big plans for huge infrastructure programs were proposed and abandoned without being executed. As a result of this situation plus the abrupt elimination of ID cards and all related functions, the world changed rapidly during the few short weeks after the first official acts of secession.

While many people longed to restore a lost way of life and would willing accept the almost suffocating stability and sweeping personal restrictions such a step would cost, a very vocal segment of the population simultaneously questioned whether the majority really wanted to go back even though some aspects of life had become quite challenging.

For Better or For Worse

John, David's close friend from David's childhood, had spent the better part of two days being frustrated and annoyed. He'd been going to the bank to get some cash the morning King's people decided to shut down access. Since then, he'd learned just how difficult meeting the basic necessities of life could be – no money for groceries and access to public places cut off because he lacked the necessary security card clearance. Even his own apartment had become off limits — despite his multitude of attempts at breaking into his own building, he only managed to fail — so he'd had to spend the time mooching off friends who'd had some cash on hand, and he was very tired of that routine.

David had been out of town for most of this headache – attending official events in Harrisburg. John was figuring he'd probably be back in town by now, so he was walking to his place in the hopes of getting some news about the current financial/security crisis and perhaps a couch he could surf that night.

John had heard just a bit of the news that morning – enough to know that David had made some sort of announcement that had people talking, which surprised John. From the fragments he'd heard, David had apparently endorsed the position that Penndelom should remain part of Pennsylvania.

Didn't sound like the David he knew to be issuing press statements . . . and John wasn't really sure he agreed with remaining part of PA. After the past two days, he just didn't trust politicians.

John was not alone in this sentiment. When the new council had voted on the issue and ended up with a five-to-five tie, that split was a pretty good reflection of the breakdown among the entire town, and emotions were getting more intense with the passage of time.

Getting no answer after knocking on David's door, John sat himself down on the steps and waited. About an hour later, he saw David and Jen walking toward him up the street.

After greeting them — and noticing the couple's relationship appeared to have become something other than purely professional — John explained his predicament.

"My couch is yours," David responded, "and the refrigerator is always open. However, you'll be pleased to know that relief is in sight."

After explaining Governor Fox's most recent update on the whole security/financial card issue, David told John about the crazy events in Harrisburg the prior night and asked whether Penndelom had experienced any attacks.

"You mean, other than protesters trying to break down the ATM machine?" John asked but then dropped the sarcasm and answered more seriously, "Some, but nothing like you've described."

"Well, have a beer and try to relax," David offered. "Meanwhile, I better call Ron Rose and bring him up to date."

Glad to be home, David was dismayed by the recent trials and tribulations relayed to him by his friend John. Always easygoing and a huge support to David in the past, he knew John would not overreact to minor inconveniences, so he got a better sense of the fallout Penndelom experienced from King's recent actions.

This train of thought was not very comforting. In fact, the weight of his own recent decisions grew immediately and made him very afraid of possible unintended consequences for his announcement.

"President King, our missions both out west and in Pennsylvania were extremely successful. No casualties on our side and just enough in so-called Southwesterly to be divisive. Reports from Pennsylvania suggest the state is in chaos."

While the president's chief of staff knew his summary was an exaggeration, he also knew his boss had a tendency to overreact, so this version was an attempt to protect King from himself.

"Are we readying another round of bombings?" King asked.

"Not yet, Sir. Seemed best to assess the situation first."

"Don't wait too long. We want to build upon the sense of danger and chaos we've already created."

"Of course, Sir."

"Fox just offered me a job," David said to Jen.

"Me, too."

"Seriously?"

"What's the job, and what are you going to tell him?" Jen asked.

"My choice of joining his election ticket as his lieutenant governor – make that COO under the new structure – or chief of staff. He's clearly crazy and doesn't know me at all. His message said my presence would secure Penndelom as part of the fold, and he noted that my name and face were now known statewide and associated with independence because of the Internet. More madness."

"So?" Jen asked again. "What will you tell him?"

"Just that. He's crazy and greatly overestimating my skill and influence. I'm going to tell him to make the same offer to Ron Rose.

That's the man he should be considering for COO or chief of staff. What about you? What job were you offered?"

"Press secretary."

"That makes perfect sense. You'd be great and are exceptionally qualified for the position he's offering you — unlike me. You should take it."

"I suspect he made my offer to help secure you," Jen said. "He seems to like the way we work together, so I'm thinking we are probably part of a package deal – you don't get one without the other."

"I kind of like the sound of us being part of a package deal."

Of all the crazy events that happened over the past few days, of all the highly uncharacteristic experiences, the only one that felt right – that he absolutely knew he wanted to explore further – was the possibility of a meaningful relationship with Jen O'Neil. He enjoyed her company but also suspected she brought out parts of his personality that usually stayed suppressed and well hidden from public view. While he hadn't a clue what she saw in him, he was choosing not to question his good fortune and believed that the interest he sensed from her really existed – unless he'd imagined just a tiny bit of unprovoked jealousy of Gretchen Moriarty, whom he'd just met.

"Yes," David added to himself, "What an interesting package that would be."

Small-town politics are a curious phenomenon. All of the players in this drama tend to be well-known to each other – very often friends, acquaintances, or enemies since childhood. A 60-year-old council woman may be greeted warmly by a contemporary from the other party, who remembers the way she dressed for Halloween in kindergarten and has memories of her as a perky high school cheerleader whose approval he sought then and still wanted now from force of habit. Consequently, a major town decision about secession or continued alliance with Pennsylvania might be influenced by two members whose teenaged feud over a girl left them incapable of voting on the same side regardless of the issue.

Such was not the case in Penndelom. While most small towns had to deal with bitter in-fighting and the minefield that is personal history and relationships, the key players in Penndelom's politics generally got along fine, tended to vote on the merits of an issue, and had the good fortune to be complemented by some younger, new additions to their ranks.

Still, votes cast by these ordinary citizens living ordinary lives in a small hamlet like Penndelom were having a huge impact upon the national – and ultimately, international – stage. This fact was too surreal for David Evans to fathom, as he was tasked with casting the deciding ballot.

David and Ron Rose met in the new Council chamber.

"So, I assume you heard we had a meeting while you were away to discuss the offer Fox made to remain part of Pennsylvania."

"How'd that go?"

"After much discussion, our straw vote ended in a five-to-five tie, which allows you to cast the deciding ballot. After reading your statement in the paper, I guess the actual vote will be just a formality."

"You annoyed, Ron? How about the rest of the Council?"

"Don't know about them yet, but I was a bit ticked off."

"Circumstances changed when King started dropping bombs," David explained.

"Fortunately for you, I've now got bigger issues on my mind. Governor Fox has contacted me about joining his election ticket as his second-in-command," Rose said. "He feels having Penndelom properly represented is very important. However, he did add one condition that should please you. Fox wants you to become the ticket's chief risk officer and mentioned that Jen O'Neil could be placed as his press secretary. I told him I thought you'd be very pleased."

"When does he need an answer?" David asked, recognizing that Fox had modified his offer to him to a slightly lesser role in going along with the suggestion to make Rose his second.

"I already told him, 'Yes,' and I said I would speak with you."

"Sorry, Ron . . . but I'm going to need a little time to digest that *and* speak with Jen."

The usual January freeze was in progress, and snow still covered all outdoor surfaces, giving the landscape a familiar appearance. However, that's where all similarity ended. Since the day King cut Pennsylvania from the computer system – and, therefore, the country – the residents' behavior had begun to change. More people could be seen in the streets at all hours of the day and night with nowhere else to go. Small groups could be found congregating on street corners, sharing whatever resources they had available – food, water, heat from open fire pits, etc.

The lights in houses and commercial buildings were mostly out – highly unusual under normal circumstances but especially for this time of year when people sought comfort indoors. Now, many who could no longer access their personal space sought shelter where possible.

In other words, the overall landscape had become increasingly desolate every day, and a sense of resigned defeat began to permeate the population – until news about the bombing of Harrisburg began to spread throughout the state.

Rather than further overwhelm the people, King's action seemed to galvanize their resolve, as anger filled the space where helplessness had been.

Cities remained dark and people still gathered to share their dwindling supplies, but a new sense of energy offered hope. When Fox reached the airways with promises that computer services would be restored soon, the citizenry's self-confidence and faith in their ability to survive apart from the U.S. was restored.

John was a perfect example of the manic/depressive mood swings experienced by the community at large. At first, he was excited to be part of a change from a way of life that had become increasingly unsuitable. Freedom from the infuriating bureaucracy of a nation devoted to a suffocating sense of security energized him and gave him greater faith in the future. Then – like so many others – John had to deal with the unexpected inconveniences and consequences of their actions. So, he no longer felt so sure of the decision.

Depressed, John had several days of despair devoted to dealing with life's necessities. Then, he heard about the bombing of Harrisburg. As he saw pictures of the attack and witnessed the state's ability to survive, his growing sense of anger was fueled by King's acts of aggression both in Pennsylvania and across the continent.

In Southwesterly, the scene was somewhat different. The moderate January climate of California, Arizona, and Nevada as well as the longer daylight hours meant the scenery was less obviously desolate. However, King's attack there had been fiercer and more widespread – and the losses much greater – so people's fear, angst, and anger were greater.

When the provisional government of Southwesterly received requests from additional states to join the alliance, the population was ready to accept them – feeling the combined resources of eight states stood a much better chance of survival.

Although no final vote had been taken, conversation seemed to center on the fact that Wyoming, Colorado, Montana, Oregon, and Washington would soon be joining the fold with many people believing Idaho would eventually almost have to follow.

This promise of increased strength propelled a growing optimism about the eventual outcome of any conflict. Decisions about the shape of the new government were well underway, though some amendments might be needed to accommodate the new members. Conversely, the few overtures made by other states to join Pennsylvania in an Eastern Alliance were rebuffed.

While Fox listened carefully to each proposal, most of them had demanded a certain amount of control over government, and the governor was unwilling to risk having the strength and innovativeness of the new constitution diluted. He was also fearful that an alliance would not be able to react quickly enough to counter any measures King might take. He knew from experience that each decision would require consensus and, therefore, compromise. Although Fox was well aware of the risks involved in taking an isolationist posture, he would rather take his chances with a more fragmented society that advanced at a much slower pace – if at all – than deal with the potential threat of a dictatorial or bureaucratic form of government.

That said, Fox was absolutely obsessed with ensuring that *all* of Pennsylvania was part of the new nation and was willing to take extra steps to bring Penndelom around prior to the PA election, which was fast approaching.

While Fox had agreed to take David Evans's advice and made Ron Rose his titular second in command, he insisted Evans have an official position even though the job he ultimately accepted was the much-diluted role of assistant deputy CEO or second in command to Rose.

Meanwhile, the rest of the world watched and waited for the outcome. The shining image of the United States had lost much of its luster over the past several decades and no longer boasted the economy or resources it once had. Other nations appeared to be in the process of developing their own posture toward current events while still maintaining a "wait and see" attitude.

"Well, the decision has been made, and the future determined for better or for worse," David said.

"Can I quote you?" Jen asked. "I'm working on my next follow-up article."

"No need to quote me; I'm nobody."

"Well then, do you mind if I steal that thought for my headline?" she continued.

"Help yourself," he agreed with a half smile.

The Council had voted again with David present, and the result was still an even split – until David cast the final ballot in favor of having Penndelom remain part of PA.

While a degree of uncertainty would always accompany any major decision, David felt quite confident that the town was making the right choice. Had they gone forward alone, they'd probably have survived just until some other government bothered to defeat and absorb them. Frankly, David felt better about the chances of Pennsylvania turning out okay and suspected that route gave Penndelom the best chance to have a voice in the world that the new nation would inhabit.

Besides, he liked and respected Fox – and maybe even trusted him a little bit.

On the eve of the PA election, David had no doubt Fox would win, and could hopefully gain support for several key issues on the ballot. Interestingly, and to his credit, Fox managed to get the state's new computer and financial systems up and running to some extent, which virtually guaranteed a victory on election day.

Daily Herald OpED

Lost Reputation
by Dr. Garfield Payne – Professor
Political Science
Penndelom Community College

While the subject of my editorial today might not seem to have the same sense of urgency as some of my previous pieces, I assure you that the stakes are very high and require immediate action.

Once upon a time, the United States was accustomed to thinking about ourselves as the dominant world power – until that belief was shaken as China finally challenged our position. Although Russia had seemed the more likely successor to us at the turn of the millennium, the dissolution of the Soviet Union and subsequent fragmentation of Eastern Europe undermined the strength and unity of that region and left them regrouping and finding a new path to continued survival.

Similarly, the perception of the U.S. has changed in the Middle East. After years of trying to weaken the U.S. through acts of terrorism used to promote political positions and ambitions, various factions no longer felt the United States was strong enough to waste time and energy on us.

In the minds of many people, this loss of international voice and prestige has significantly accelerated in recent years. Foreign leaders no longer believe in our word, promises, or intentions and clearly consider us a fading superpower. A new parochialism has taken hold in our country, and others have noticed the difference.

While some smaller, weaker countries still seem to pay lip service to the United States, we can delude ourselves and pretend we are still dominant. Although France, England, Italy, Greece, and even immediate neighbors such as Mexico and Canada might officially be deferential to us, I have personally noticed a difference in the way regular citizens have interacted with me while traveling abroad. They clearly no longer feel a need to treat me or other visitors from the U.S. as special. They no longer behave like poor relations whose presence is being graced by a visiting rich Uncle Sam.

So, what does all this mean on a practical level?

Recognizing the damage that had been done to the reputation of the nation, Southwesterly has already begun reaching out to foreign powers in an effort to establish its own identity and cultivate new, separate relations apart from the United States. Frankly, I believe this action is both wise and necessary, and I encourage our other newly founded government coalitions to follow their lead.

"Out Foxed"

While the attack on Pennsylvania by the United States certainly shook up residents, the bombing also strengthened their resolve. No packed cars left town. No exodus occurred. Instead, the areas that received greatest destruction were cleaned up and made habitable. Fortunately, unlike Southwesterly, no lives had been lost!

Nevertheless, damage had been done, and the landscape was scarred by the attack. Perhaps not coincidentally, voting for the new PA government officials occurred at a location next to a bomb crater too deep to be easily filled.

Voter turnout was exceedingly high – the highest in decades. People once again felt their voice might actually make a difference in the outcome. That said, the results were all but a forgone conclusion. Fox had always been very popular and was now seen as the second coming of George Washington – father of their new country. Most of the members running with him were familiar faces with Ron Rose and David Evans being the newcomers. However, David was highly recognizable from his Internet exposure and extremely popular – especially after his much-publicized exploits during the bombing. Ron Rose was essentially an unknown but one who carried a Fox/Evans endorsement.

Consequently, election results were posted with modest fanfare, though audiences everywhere paid close attention to Fox's acceptance speech.

He reiterated the new roles that would do the work of government and gave all his reasons for believing a business model made sense. He explained that the Board of Directors would provide an ultimate check and balance over the new CEO while further serving in a meaningful watch-dog capacity.

He closed his speech with an optimistic vision of the future and a challenge: "King – if you are listening – the Independent Nation of Pennsylvania is undeterred by your bombs and your cowardly temper tantrums. We are building an exciting new nation. When the day comes that you will beg to join us, we *will* remember."

In recent days, John had learned to find his sources of excitement in different places. This morning, not believing but having no choice, he went to the bank as Fox had suggested he do in his victory speech the night before.

So, buttoning his thin coat – a handout from a displacement center – against the cold January wind, he joined a long line that was moving very slowly but making some progress. Spirits were, in fact, exceptionally high among the crowd as John, along with everyone else, realized it was true; people could once again access their money at an almost fully functional bank.

Now, John was on his way to his apartment building and was expecting to get inside – longing for a shower, pot of coffee, and change of clothes – the simple pleasures!

The speech by Fox last night told people about the progress that had been made in restoring a government computer system. While not the same one, this new alternative was a functional construct that could manage and address the needs of daily life without picking up the crippling bureaucracy and paranoid sense of security that had become the United States.

John was a fan and a believer, especially after Ron Rose and David joined the ticket. He wondered how Fox had managed that feat and could only imagine the kind of carrot he must have dangled to get David to agree.

Swiping his card in the keylock and hearing that wonderful click of a door ready to be opened, John felt day one of the new nation under the leadership of Fox was off to an auspicious start! After grabbing some much-needed sleep in the comfort of his own home, the perfect way to spend a few hours on this cold, late-January day, he'd tried to track down Jen and David.

At the request of the newly elected Pennsylvania "CEO," David and Ron Rose traveled back to Harrisburg by helicopter to be formally introduced to the rest of the state and the other members of the new administration. This time, Jen stayed behind to finish her story for the newspaper, a parting that was surprisingly difficult.

"Congratulations, gentlemen," Fox said to David and Ron Rose. "Nice victory."

"Right back at you," Ron responded. "Where do we start?"

"We have lots of work ahead," Fox warned, "including drafting a new constitution and working with the elected department heads to get their units within our government up and running. However – as important as such initiatives are – I think the first order of business needs to be securing the peace. We must stop King's random, unprovoked attacks before we experience loss of life."

"And how do you plan to do that?" Rose asked. "We have no organized military yet."

"Old-fashioned diplomacy."

"Were you any good at the board game?" David quipped.

"The best!" Fox responded. "I've got a plan."

He then went on to explain that all the states flocking to join the Southwesterly alliance had made King extremely angry and nervous – a useful combination for PA. "We still have people within the White House who remain loyal to us," he said. "That's the reason we can know for sure just how truly unbalanced King has become. Anyway, his fear of the Southwesterly union has already prompted worse attacks than we experienced, and more will follow. King knows that several states have approached Pennsylvania about forming our own Northeasterly alliance, and he is angry and afraid of that possibility."

"You've already very wisely decided not to go down that road," David said.

"Yes, but King does not know that," Fox answered, "and probably cannot fathom a mindset that would even consider preferring to remain small and self-contained."

"Basically," David concluded with a smile, "you are planning to out-fox him."

"Exactly," Fox said, enjoying the pun. "PA will promise not to enter into any alliance agreements with neighboring states in return for a commitment to cease aggression and formally acknowledge PA's independence. From his point of view, the deal will seem safe because he'll think we are promising to keep ourselves small and weak."

"You think he'll actually go for that?"

"He cares more about the west and now has limited resources. He knows he can't fight battles on both sides of the country. World War II showed everyone the stupidity of that course of action. Besides, he's going to *want* to believe me. So yes, I think King will jump at that offer of a treaty, figuring he can resume hostilities further down the road after he's dealt with Southwesterly. However, that buys us lots of time to get our act together and develop long-range plans for dealing with King."

The scene at the Oval Office was one of jubilation.

"My plan to squash Pennsylvania has worked," King smugly stated. "They've come crawling back to me to beg for no more bombs. In return, they are willing to give up their future."

"Congratulations, Sir."

"Can you believe they are willing to sacrifice any hope of becoming large and strong? They are willing to remain a broken, impoverished little postage stamp in the vast expanse of North America just because they are suddenly afraid."

"So, you plan to sign the treaty?"

"Indeed, and I will be sure our former friends in Southwesterly understand the implications for them. In fact, contact Fox. Tell him we want the treaty signed in a formal ceremony broadcast across the planet. I'm sure our allies in Europe and Asia will find this announcement interesting."

David

"Ready to head home?" Ron Rose asked.

"More than ready," David replied. He'd done his duty and was now anxious to get back. He knew he'd have to return to Harrisburg for the official treaty signing that King had requested, but at least Jen would be able to accompany him on that trip.

The flight normally took under an hour on such a clear day, but David felt restless. He felt a sense of unease he attributed to too much time spent on tasks he didn't like in new settings that made him uncomfortable. Trying hard to take his mind off the present moment, he shook his head in disbelief as he considered who he had become — a politician, heading home on a helicopter, after a meeting with the head of the new Independent Nation of Pennsylvania.

He'd had a pretty idyllic childhood growing up in Penndelom. The city was small enough for children to have quite a lot of safe, personal freedom. As a result, he and his friends spent lots of time playing sports, inventing creative versions of hide-and-seek, and just hanging out while exploring the neighborhood.

While David had a large group of childhood friends, he remained on the periphery because he happened to be several years younger at an age when even a year made a huge difference. However, he was tall and athletic, so he was allowed to be part of that older group, who happened to regularly need an extra person – essential when picking teams.

Being the youngest of this pack helped shape David's personality. He became accustomed to being the last chosen. He also got used to not having his voice heard. So, he learned to watch and listen but generally kept his opinions to himself.

Nevertheless, David was not uncomfortable with his place among the group, and he enjoyed getting to participate in their activities, which suited him better than those of his peers. Days were spent outdoors – including many hours in a tall tree house overlooking the field where they played.

Spring and summer meant baseball, while fall meant football. Winter brought sledding as well as ice skating and hockey at a nearby lake.

This pattern of life continued for much of David's elementary school experience – until all his older friends moved up to middle school, leaving him behind to find his own ways to fill the void.

John was David's close friend from the start. Though he was not allowed to be part of the older kids' group, he and David spent a lot of time together. When the elder kids moved on, John was extremely helpful in introducing David to the world of their contemporaries. However, being on the outskirts much of his early life taught David to be self-reliant. He never felt like he truly fit in with either group, and he became accustomed to dealing with a low-grade, but on-going, feeling of loneliness.

David was a surprise to his parents, being born while they were both in their mid-40's, 10 years after his sister, who was his only other sibling. This meant David was given quite a bit of freedom by parents whose energy had already been drained.

Despite that, David always felt loved and protected, and he was quite close to his sister regardless of the difference in their ages.

Although David was very gifted academically, he seemed for some reason to go out of his way to hide this fact. More often than not, he found good grades and lots of attention to be a barrier to friendships, rather than an invitation. While he never sabotaged his success in school, he simply did not advertise his accomplishments and made a point of not participating in class. By the time he was halfway through middle school, his friendship with John and prowess on the basketball team gave him sufficient entry into various circles of public-school society.

College changed some of David's habits of interacting with his world but did not change him. The lessons were already too ingrained.

He became a historian. Always fascinated by the past, David studied and enjoyed writing about days gone by – feeling that lots of lessons helpful in moving forward could still be learned by looking back.

He was a sophomore at Penn State University when both of his parents died within a month of each other. First, his mother fell victim to cancer; then, his father passed away shortly thereafter. Although the death certificate listed a heart attack as the cause, David always believed the real culprit was grief.

David's on-going sense of loneliness grew worse, even with his sister's generous efforts to involve him in her life. With her help and John's, he survived, despite some extreme reclusiveness.

Finally, during his senior year, David met Mary Strand, who helped pull him back into a fairly normal life and interaction with the world. Comfortable is the word David would use to describe his relationship with Mary, and he was pretty sure she felt the same. They were generally compatible and shared many interests and opinions – qualities David found to be helpful in reintegrating himself into the world.

When they finally had sex that, too, felt comfortable; it was a deeper connection that was warm and welcoming . . . but not explosive.

They enjoyed a very pleasant senior year together, and most people assumed their relationship was a permanent one. At graduation, Mary announced that she had won a scholarship abroad and would be leaving for France in the summer.

She asked David to visit, but she did not ask him to join her.

That's when David decided he better return to Penndelom, at least for a while.

Finding few jobs – make that *no* jobs – for historians, David picked up some audiovisual work. He'd always been a bit of an A/V geek and was good at handling equipment, so he slipped easily into the role without any real training. That's pretty much the life he was leading when he'd been asked to do some setup for the announcement of Penndelom's withdrawal from the union.

The morning he'd met Jen marked a turning point in his life for a number of reasons. When he was around her – or even just thinking about her – he no longer felt that constant, low-grade sense of loneliness. This change hadn't happened throughout his entire relationship with Mary. Having felt that way virtually every day of his life up to this point, he was suddenly free of a weight he did not even realize he'd been carrying.

Never overly interested in politics, though he certainly did have political views, David was puzzled by the events that appeared determined to sweep him into this unfamiliar world.

Having gone through three decades without even voting much of the time, he suddenly found himself holding a political office. Admittedly, the job was his way of compromising between what Fox had wanted and what he was willing to do — but it was still a government position as part of an elected ticket, nonetheless.

With an A/V job that kept landing him in very visible places, David was not sure how to extricate himself from politics. Oddly enough, he recently began to wonder whether or not he should try. Frankly, he *did* think Penndelom was wise to secede but was even more convinced that the city was far better off remaining part of Pennsylvania – especially with a pretty good man like Governor Fox at the helm. Besides, he was in a role not likely to have any kind of meaningful input within this culture.

When David was young, he was fairly adept at embracing new experiences and seemed to be able to adapt quite readily. That is — until his mom passed away. Nothing he did could help her, and despite all his efforts to keep his dad engaged in life, he lost his father a few short weeks later. Both were unexpected and unwanted events that created a feeling of helplessness that was quite new and would never again completely leave him.

Any event that he was not personally able to manage left him with a fear of his life, once again, spinning out of control. Although it was misguided logic, to avoid such moments, David simply started limiting his number of new experiences so he might stand a better chance of at least keeping a hand in his own destiny. The sense of life leading him, rather than him leading life, eventually did somewhat subside. However, his attitude toward the unknown never completely left him.

Touching down in Penndelom, David was pleased to see that Jen had come to meet the helicopter.

"David," said Ron, "we better make our report to the council. While the function of our newly elected group is unclear now that we are remaining part of PA, I assume that body – *we* – will be responsible for setting up a local Penndelom government to interact with the state."

"What do you say we give ourselves a break tonight, Ron? Tomorrow will be soon enough."

"You're right," Ron said with a tired sigh. "We'll meet with the council tomorrow. 9 a.m."

On their walk to his apartment, David described for Jen the scene in Harrisburg – everything from the election and the crowd's reaction to Fox's acceptance speech to the puzzled response to the appointment of David and Ron Rose. He concluded with Fox's plan for a treaty to give Pennsylvania some time to get organized as a free country before having to deal with King.

"Clever plan," Jen commented. "Seems to be working. Fortunately for us, he's one smart guy."

Arriving home, David found his old security card now unlocked his door. He read a note from John thanking him for his help and indicating that he could once again access his bank account and apartment. As a result, he'd left a bottle of wine to express his appreciation.

"So, Jen," David said, "what do you say we also make a deal. For the rest of the night, no more talk about politics, the world crises, the future of PA, or the fortunes of Penndelom. Just the two of us in a bubble."

"Sounds wonderful, but what will we have left to say to each other?"

"Let's find out," David said as he found two glasses and opened the wine. They settled down on his couch, watching the flames of his small fireplace as they shared life stories. The moments that made them happy, those that made them sad, and all points in between. During a lull in the conversation, Jen noticed they had finished the wine. "I think I have another bottle somewhere," David said as he started to rise. With a hand on his thigh, Jen stopped him, saying, "I have a better idea." She leaned over and gently caught his lips with hers. What started off tender was soon fueled by passion as all thoughts of wine — and clothing — were forgotten. Gazing at Jen's naked form, David knew he never had, and would likely never again, see a more beautiful sight.

Their joining felt like the most natural thing in the world to them. Their bodies intertwined, welcoming each other home and moving as one, until they were both exhausted and content. As their breathing returned to normal, they looked into each other's eyes, both finding a softer, more intimate expression than either had ever experienced before. Any doubt one might have had about the other was now completely a part of the past.

A few hours later, still on the couch and wide awake— unlike Jen— he watched the slow, steady rise and fall of her chest as she slept.

Eventually, her eyes gradually opened, and her lips curved into a soft smile.

"Hi there, Mr. Evans," she said. "That was quite a performance."

"Would you like an encore?"

She cocked one eyebrow and asked in a serious tone, "Are you sure you're up for it?" Then she let out a squeal of laughter as he suddenly rolled them both off the couch and onto the floor.

Their futures became intertwined that night; separate paths into separate futures no longer existed. Both of them were happy, relieved, and looking forward to tomorrow with a greater sense of optimism.

Seeing the first light of dawn starting to peak through the window, Jen put on David's shirt and nearly danced her way to the kitchen. She understood that she had technically only known David for a few days, but they had packed a lot of living, sharing, and emotion into that time. She felt as though she had always known him.

He was quiet, reserved, thoughtful, and caring. He possessed all those qualities and so much more, including being charismatic enough to draw attention in a crowd without doing anything particularly extroverted.

She knew times were changing. The whole world was suddenly shifting and yet she felt safe when she was with him.

As David stirred, she brought him a cup of coffee. She looked lovely in his shirt, so after he took a sip, he commented, "I don't remember you asking permission to wear that shirt."

With a twinkle in her eye, Jen replied, "Well then, I suppose I'll just have to take it off."

The size of his grin spoke volumes as he said, "That's much better. Now — come here."

By the time they finished, dawn was no longer breaking, and the coffee was cold.

Not wanting the night to end, David and Jen slowly got dressed. As they did, he debated telling her a story about his parents that he thought might help her to understand who he was a bit better.

Deciding to go ahead, he started off by letting her know the incident was not dramatic, but a telling one. While he had not yet been born at the time, the story itself left an indelible imprint on him.

"My mother's cousin and her husband had money and were very attuned to slight differences in social strata. This one night, the four of them had been out for dinner. As they were leaving, a mutual acquaintance spotted them and walked over.

'I didn't realize the four of you knew each other,' the person said — a person, I might add, who had even more money and social influence than my mother's cousin.

'Eleanor and I are related,' my mother said.

'Jeremy and I thought we'd take them to a fancy restaurant,' my mother's cousin announced, clearly indicating that the four of them did not regularly socialize while simultaneously acknowledging that my parents had less money and social rank.

'Oh,' my father said, 'you thought that was fancy?'

My father and mother supposedly exchanged a knowing glance, according to my mother's version, when he casually mentioned that my mother had taught the mutual acquaintance's children.

'And they loved her class,' the woman remarked. 'That year was a difficult one for us, what with my miscarriage and my mother passing away. Our life was very unsettled, which our children apparently felt as they suddenly became discipline problems. They seemed to find some catharsis in school, and our daughter loved doing writing assignments for your class. She seemed to find a much-needed release.'

Conversation fully steered from Eleanor and Jeremy's money and status to a place they could not go. I think my mother felt they had gotten the upper hand that night, and my father had the final word in a bitter, lifelong, and unproductive rivalry between cousins."

David paused for a moment before he tried to explain. "I was never sure why that story was … is … always so poignant for me." He said, "Perhaps I was reacting to the glances they used to share whenever the story was recounted. But now, I think I realize that it's because my father understood my mother so well. He recognized a need she had — that she would refuse to address — and managed to take care of the situation in a manner that she would find acceptable and that did not involve any actions on her part." He took care of her, and she did the same for him in countless similar ways. They were a team. My sister and I were the beneficiaries. But that also means they set a pretty high bar for the way a relationship should be." Feeling a bit self-conscious, he concluded with, "Why I'm telling you this story now, I do not know. Guess something about recent events made me feel that sharing the memory with you was important."

Jen lightly touched the side of his face, brushed her lips against his, and with a little smile, softly said, "Thank you."

"Can I fix you supper back here tonight?" Jen asked as they left the apartment.

"Only if I can bring the wine," David said with a knowing smile.

Barely blushing, she responded, "I've got a story to write, and you and Ron have a town meeting.

"You're right, but I'll still be looking forward to our dinner," he said. Then, he traced a finger down her cheek, lifted her chin, and gave her a gentle kiss – smiling as he walked away, hoping he had given her something to look forward to as well.

The Battle of Pennsylvania

The day started the way so many had over the past month with the news reporting the latest incident – a word most people heard as "battle" – between U.S. President King and Southwesterly. At first, all the aggression had been on the part of King, trying a number of different strategies to weaken the new union. As each effort was easily defeated, Southwesterly gained confidence and began some initiatives of their own aimed at driving their old boss and his followers from their land. The tipping point that ultimately caused Southwesterly to become more proactive and daring happened when King tried and failed to do a major missile launch without the necessary expertise, and every one missed the mark. While Southwesterly was more successful than not, King's presence could still be felt.

Meanwhile, Pennsylvania was making every effort to use the time wisely. While King's attention was diverted, the independent government was put into place. The newly elected officials began staffing their departments as the constitution was drafted, discussed, modified, and gradually hammered into a workable form that suited the needs of each discipline, stayed within Fox's original vision, and was left ambiguous enough to change and evolve over time as circumstances dictated.

David was more involved in the process than he would have anticipated given the "helper" nature of his job and title. He attended every meeting but saw his duty as assisting Ron Rose and perhaps offering some advice. However, Fox did recruit him for a few particular projects that David found to be interesting and challenging . . . so he was glad to be involved.

While he could not yet tell how the new government was faring, David was impressed by the unexpected spirit of cooperation everyone seemed to bring to the task.

David believed Fox had learned to view Ron Rose as more of an asset than a liability. Ron, to his credit, seemed to be treating his job with the right spirit and not allowing his ego to interfere with his role.

Fox's vision of a modified business model was getting put into place with each of the functional department heads having enormous responsibility for defining, developing, and executing the processes within their groups. Once the CFO's Finance unit was up and running – having successfully adapted old systems to continue operating separate from the huge United States' computer servers— the chief risk officer was next in line to get the most attention. Everyone knew security and defense were critical with King located just around the corner and continuing to be a bully with a chip on his shoulder. Everyone also knew Pennsylvania owed Southwesterly a debt of gratitude for occupying King's attention at a critical time.

Jen liked her new position as press secretary. Much of it could be done remotely and she was excited to be part of events destined to become a new chapter in future history books.

As the need to keep the public informed about the evolution of PA grew, more staff was added, and her specialty became reporting on the activities of Fox, Rose, and the Board of Directors. Others in her group did

Finance, Risk, Operations, etc.

Life gradually seemed to be slipping into a much-needed routine. Although habits formed now were destined to go away once King turned his attention in their direction, Pennsylvania could at least indulge in this moment of quiet respite to regroup and recharge depleted batteries.

Perhaps the happiest person at this more positive turn of events was John. Back in his own place with money in hand, able to return to work, he epitomized the trend witnessed everywhere – people relieved to rediscover the simple joys of a place to stay, food to eat, and fresh clothes to wear.

He started cooking instead of living on take-out, and he made a point of introducing himself to his neighbors. He rescued a cocker spaniel from the local chapter of the S.P.C.A. and walked the pup through the streets of his neighborhood, instead of working out in isolation at the gym. While he knew this peaceful interlude might not last, he was determined not to waste a single moment.

John made a point of regularly visiting David and Jen, who were now living together. He envied their relationship but felt sorry his friend had to deal with the current role he'd had thrust upon him. Through no fault of his own, the guy was pushed into a more public role than John would have ever envisioned for him. While he knew David hated this highly public position, John also knew David was inexplicably good at such jobs. Perhaps he excelled because he *didn't* like them and did not *want* the notoriety. He certainly was not jockeying for even more of the same.

Walking to the grocery store, relieved to know the shelves would be fully stocked, John reminded himself that he better make arrangements with David and Jen – funny how the two names now rolled off the tongue as one – to take care of his dog, Fala, should his unit get called up.

John was a long-term member of the National Guard, a decision he made when fresh out of high school to get an education and have some much-needed early income. When Pennsylvania seceded from the United States, the reserves became Pennsylvania's army, and he fully expected to be called to active duty. While some of his friends and fellow reservists would not show up – contending that they never signed up for a full-time military position, especially one for just Pennsylvania – John actually believed in the new country and wanted to do his part.

All in all, the separate Independent Nation of Pennsylvania was off to a good start with the bleak months of January and February behind them. Tomorrow was March 1st – St. David's Day for the Welsh, which included John's mother whose maiden name was Llwellyn as she often reminded him – with the official start of spring just a few short weeks away.

On his way to David and Jen's, John hoped they might have some news that could convince him that further conflict might possibly be avoided. He was not anxious to don his uniform again.

Knocking on the door – pup on a leash beside him – John entered when David hollered. "Come on in! I want to see that puppy!"

"Sorry to disturb you," he said as he closed the door behind him, "but I was just up the street."

"You never need a reason, and I'm not disturbed."

"That's arguable," John joked.

"How about a cup of coffee or a coke?"

"Nothing . . .except maybe some good news for a change. What's happening in Harrisburg?"

"Making progress," David answered. "Feels slow, but I guess that's inevitable."

"So, do you think King's going to come after us, too? Just wondering whether I should expect my unit to be activated."

"I haven't heard any news to that effect, but you know King as well as I do. What do *you* think?"

"He'll be coming after us."

"Right."

"I guess the real question is – how soon?"

Before David could answer, Jen entered and began making a fuss over the dog.

"When I need to report, can I leave my pup with you until I get back?"

"Of course," Jen said without hesitation. "Love to have him. Does that mean you've gotten your notice?"

"No. Just getting prepared and expect I'll have to move fast when the time comes. Meanwhile, he and I were out enjoying a walk on this nice sunny day, happy the snow is almost gone everywhere." Then, changing topics, John asked, "What are your thoughts about Fox now?"

David paused before replying, "A very smart man and a very good person, which I consider a rare and winning combination. I trust him, and I can't say that about too many people."

"We going to be able onto hang onto this new world of ours and make the darn thing work?" John asked.

"We stand a pretty good chance . . . until we get greedy and screw up. As we all know, the main cause is usually greed."

"Now, David," Jen rebuked, "let's be optimistic."

"Assume you heard about those states that wanted to form an alliance with us," David remarked, "until Fox turned them down."

"No. What?" John asked.

"All of New England plus New York have formed their own alliance and a country called Northeasterly."

"Gee, what a clever name," John's words were thick with sarcasm. "I wonder where they got the idea?"

"No formal announcement has been made quite yet – but this news is not exactly a secret. Seems like defense and security are their primary motivations. They plan to figure out their new form of government at a later date but seemed determined to remain the same as much as possible."

"This latest development must be driving King nuts," John responded. "He's had very little success against Southwesterly, and this new group is much closer – basically in his own backyard. Now I know I'm getting called up soon, so I'll be sure to get some dog food, a bed, some treats, and a few toys for you to have on hand."

Several quiet days passed. The weather was getting warmer with crocuses and daffodils starting to poke early shoots through the ground.

On the 15th of the month — the Ides of March – King made his move.

What was unexpected, was that he began his first eastern assault against Pennsylvania instead the Northeasterly states.

Some theorists speculated King finally realized his treaty with Fox had yielded him nothing and threw a tantrum like a spoiled child. Others figured Pennsylvania was just a large geographical obstacle between Washington D.C. and his real targets to the north. In other words, he was clearing the way for ground troop movements. Given his past experience negotiating with Fox, King didn't even try to get PA to agree to open the border to the United States.

The attack was multifaceted and began with missiles launched at Harrisburg. However, King's troops were once again off target. Instead of the capitol, the rockets landed on and around Middletown – the site of the historical Three Mile Island nuclear disaster. Though the power plant had been shut down a long time ago, the residents retained scars from having heard countless stories over the years about both the incident and the years of post-traumatic stress that followed.

Meanwhile, ground troops – expecting that the missiles had cleared the way for their ground attack – headed toward both Harrisburg and Philadelphia. With the latter being a harbor town, King also sent the navy to attack by sea.

Foot soldiers found themselves facing more of a philosophical crisis than the damage caused by artillery that had been launched from afar. The men and women fighting on the ground seemed to suddenly realize they were pointing weapons at former fellow citizens. In some cases, perhaps even relatives from the neighboring state.

While a number of units mutinied and refused to bear arms, others simply moved *very* slowly – perhaps hoping fate might intervene and call off this whole unfortunate decision.

"My unit's been called up," John said as soon as David answered the knock on his door.

"I have to head to Harrisburg," David replied, "but Jen will be here. Besides, the dog likes her better anyway."

"I'd have thought Fox would be clearing out of the city," John observed.

"No, he's gathering all of his resources to the capitol," David responded. Then, he looked his friend in the eye and said "Please be careful, John. You know I've lost far too many people from my life already."

"That goes for you, too, Buddy. Don't know exactly what you'll be doing, but Harrisburg is a hot spot right now, and you've been developing a proclivity for landing smack in the middle of whatever crazy event happens to be occurring at the moment."

Life was once again spinning hopelessly out of his control as David watched John slowly walk away, his confused dog whimpering softly at David's side.

Refusing to even contemplate the possibility of never seeing John again, David tried desperately to close his mind to any negative thoughts – fearful that to think them might somehow make them happen.

Stooping to comfort John's pup and trying not to be melancholy about memories from their childhood, he was faced with knowing the war with the United States had yet again assumed a new level of reality. As he stood and stared out his window, David saw John raise his hand without turning around, receding into the distance as he continued to wave, knowing that David would continue to watch long afterward.

"I'm glad you've got the dog to keep you company," David said as he made sure he had everything he needed for the trip to the capitol.

"Don't be stupid." Jen said as she held him close before giving him a parting kiss to remember.

"Do I look stupid?"

"Well . . ." She responded. "Just try to be careful and be smart. Fox told the press and communications staff to keep working remotely."

"I'm glad to hear it. I expect Fox, and the people he's gathering together, will be out of harm's way."

"You somehow manage to get yourself into the middle of things. I don't know how a wallflower like you makes that happen."

"I don't go looking. Stuff just finds me."

"Please don't make those famous last words."

As the helicopter touched down, David and Ron Rose disembarked and got into a van taking people to the staging area Fox had set up just outside the city.

"Never saw this coming. Figured Northeasterly would be the next target," Rose said. By the way, I heard John and his platoon are headed to Philly to help shore up their defenses."

"Any idea what *we're* supposed to be doing?" David asked.

"I imagine join in discussions about military strategies and participate in votes about the allocation of resources."

The van, carrying five members of the Fox administration and its driver, was speeding along Route 81 when one of King's many misguided missiles struck the highway in front of them.

Although the vehicle was not directly hit by the missile, the force from the explosion, coupled with the damage to the road, caused it to flip over.

The driver, the new chief of education, and Ron Rose were all killed.

David and the other two survivors climbed free of the debris from the badly damaged van.

"We should wait by the vehicle," said one man whose arm appeared to be broken. "It will be easily spotted, and our people are probably already aware that we've had a problem."

"Let's see whether we can get through on the phone." David offered. "If not, I suggest we leave a message for any would-be rescuers and start walking. We're only about a mile and a half from where we were heading. Less, as the crow flies."

David's phone was miraculously undamaged, so he set the GPS for their presumed destination, and they slowly set off. In addition to the man with the broken arm, the other had an injury to his ankle, causing him to limp. They all had scrapes and bruises, but David was lucky to have no issues other than that.

Along the way, they saw that a school had been hit. Fortunately, all sessions had been cancelled in anticipation of possible actions from King, so the structure was empty. A little further on, they came across an office building that had been demolished, and they added three more people to their ranks. The scene was played out numerous times as they traveled, and the little band gradually grew to 50 survivors of King's misguided missiles, nearly all with some sort of injuries.

After what felt like several hours of walking, hobbling, and shuffling along, David and his band of already war-weary misfits arrived at their destination, where they were greeted at the door by the familiar and very welcomed sight of Gretchen Moriority.

"David Evans!" she said with obvious relief. "Your message was found at the crash site, but we had no vehicles to send for you." She looked past him to the crowd of people behind him and added, "I was told to expect *three* of you."

"We made some friends along the way, and every one of us is a casualty of King's military actions gone awry."

"I'll see your friends get situated," Gretchen said. "Please know I'm very sorry about Ron Rose and the others. Unfortunately, I've got to take you to Fox right now. We can catch up later."

She nodded to her left as she said, "By the way, David, that news photographer over there has been waiting to take pictures of the three of you survivors returning. I'd venture to say he's already got his shots, and your group will be Internet celebrities for the next few days."

Gretchen half-smiled apologetically at David's frown.

On route to meet with Fox, David called Jen to tell her about Ron Rose.

Shocked . . . and then choked up, she commented, "So that makes you Fox's new deputy."

"I suppose that's the way succession would work, though I'm on my way to meet with Fox now. How's the pup?"

"We've *got* to get one, David!" she gushed.

"Going that well," he softly chuckled. "We'll see. Gotta go. I'll talk to you later."

"I'm very sorry about Ron Rose," Fox said. "I was just getting to know – *and* like – him. Such a freak accident."

"The only 'accident' was regarding King's aim," he responded.

"I know you were initially reluctant, but you do realize, don't you, that you now have to take over his role."

"Yes. I was afraid that might be the case. I'm not exactly overjoyed, but I will do the best I can."

"I know you will." Fox remarked. After a pause, he continued, "We've had some good news. Southwesterly is fed up with King and is willing to mount an attack on the United States."

"What's the catch?" David asked.

"They said they are ready and willing, as long as their assault is choreographed with an equal commitment from us to begin an offensive on Washington D.C."

"Ah ..."

"They don't want us to wait until King decides he's ready to eliminate us. Unfortunately, I don't know whether we are ready to mount a long-distance offensive yet. All of our military actions so far have been defensive and close to home, as well as close to our supply chain."

"Let's get Northeasterly to help us do our part. It would be in their best interest *and* ours."

"Not a bad suggestion, David. Think you can make that happen?"

"I can try," he responded. "I've heard Northeasterly is currently based in Boston. I can leave in a couple of hours."

"Take the helicopter."

"Our leverage is the chance to have Southwesterly and us to help them fight their battles. Conflict is inevitable for them – only a matter of time. By moving now, they get lots of proven assistance. I think they might go for that."

Arriving in Boston, David and the pilot disembarked. Given King's actions, they were greeted by several armed guards.

Currently, Northeasterly's ad hoc government was housed on the campus of Harvard in Cambridge. Seeing lots of red brick everywhere, David felt he was in the presence of history and was hoping to create more. After making his way to the correct hallway, on the correct floor, and in the correct building, he finally knocked on what he hoped was the correct office door. The knock was answered by a gentleman who said, "Greetings," and waved him into the room, where a woman was already seated on the office couch. They appeared to be the two Northeasterly government representatives he had been told to meet – a senator and secretary of development – who were obviously expecting him.

The woman smiled and said, "We understand you are on an important mission."

"We believe so," David agreed and proceeded to tell them the state of affairs as he knew them. "Bottom line," he concluded, "we have a brief set of circumstances that can serve all of our interests extremely well. However, our window of opportunity will be short-lived, and we will need to act quickly for this to work. We can defeat him once and for all, and we can drive him from our lands. Or …" David let his comment trail off into silence.

"When?" the woman asked David.

"Tomorrow. The window is closing, and King still has some foreign allies willing to come to his aid."

David and the two Northeasterly government officials — the man was now identified as the senator — explained the situation to a larger group. By the time they were finished, he had their full agreement and was headed back to Harrisburg the same day.

The attack on King and the remaining portion of the United States was set to commence in eight hours.

After his formal debriefing with Fox and the Board, David was told, "Outstanding job. You've got a future in government!" added Fox. "I doubt anyone else — myself included — could have done as well."

"I can't explain much over the phone," David said when he called Jen that evening, "but I will not be home tomorrow. You and the rest of the communications team will likely be getting the low-down shortly. I suggest you keep your phone close by, so you don't miss that call. Fox has secure lines and can be more forthcoming." Pausing, he then added, "I miss my nice, comfortable bed, and the one who keeps it warm."

"Sorry, but I've got a new bed buddy – one with absolutely dreamy eyes."

"Yeah. Yeah. I know. And he has four short, hairy legs plus a tail that's constantly wagging. Just lay low and stay close to home tomorrow," David was doing his best to warn her without compromising military secrecy.

"*You're* telling *me* to lay low," Jen laughed. "You, whose face is splashed across the Internet every other day along side your latest exploits."

"Not my fault."

"That's the irony," she half-smiled and then made *him* promise to lay low.

After they said good night, David let his thoughts return to the matter at hand — realizing that twenty-four hours from now, the battle of Pennsylvania will not only have begun but will hopefully have been won.

The night was clear, still, and quite warm for late winter/early spring. A full moon lit a wide path across the landscape as the first Pennsylvania troops moved out for Washington. The plan was for them to meet up with Northeasterly's infantry in Maryland, coinciding with a series of air strikes by the newly allied parties.

David knew that soon, a scene from "The Star-Spangled Banner" would be re-enacted with rockets' red glare ... and bombs bursting in air; only instead of marking the beginning of the union, those words would be marking the beginning of the end.

Startled by his phone ringing in the middle of the night, David felt a bit wary when he saw the caller was Fox.

"Hello?"

"David, I know you just got back from Boston, but I'm going to ask you to hit the road again. I need you to be my eyes and ears. With all the action focused on Washington, I want a presence in that general vicinity just in case some need arises. Whether you can check in with us or not at the time, you have my proxy to make decisions and speak on my behalf."

Although he said, "Of course," he felt unsure of what he was being asked to do. Before he could get more details, Fox said, "Transportation has been arranged to take you to the designated location." He added, "I'll be in touch," and then he hung up.

Feeling weary but wide awake from a surge of adrenalin, David could only hope that his role would become clearer in time.

The first shots had already been fired by the time David arrived in Baltimore and had met up with the same two Northeasterly representatives from yesterday. The three of them got updated briefings every 30 minutes and watched footage from the web cams mounted on the helmets of many of the soldiers. Thus far, the battle seemed to be going well. King's troops in Washington appeared to have been caught unawares. David suspected King was just now understanding which parties were participating in the attack against him and the rest of the United States.

"Pennsylvania and Southwesterly *and* those new traitors are all banding together?" King repeated in utter disbelief.

"Yes, Mr. President. Quite unprecedented."

"Have we mounted a counteroffensive yet?"

"General Southland was killed. I'm not sure who is taking command locally."

"Get General Johnson on the line."

"Yes, Sir," his aid responded just as a missile struck the West Wing of the White House.

Chaos erupted as splintered wood and demolished furniture rained down, igniting fires in other areas. The sprinkler system was triggered, adding to the smoke and fumes as water hit the burning contents of the rooms. A strong stench of sulfur caused anyone within dozens of feet to cough, sneeze, and gag. Half of the White House had been obliterated, and a security team searched the rubble of the Oval Office to try to determine whether President King had been at his desk at the time of the attack.

While only one well-placed missile had done this damage to the White House, the sound and vibrations of other explosions rocked key targets throughout the city, and emergency sirens could soon be heard in all directions. The National Mall, that tranquil pool of water and manicured park between the Lincoln Memorial and the Capitol Building, had been quickly designated as the staging area for King's counteroffensive until that landmark was also struck by a bomb.

Doing their best to get a portion of the White House staff and key personnel to a safe location, a caravan of secure and heavily armored black SUVs – that were always kept in a state of readiness and led by one nicknamed "The Beast" – was in the process of transporting a group to Camp David in Maryland when they also came under fire and were pinned down upon finding one road after another impassable due to craters. While Marine One – the president's helicopter – had landed on the White House lawn waiting for passengers to board, President King was nowhere to be found.

The battle raged on throughout the night – on the ground, in the air, and by sea – challenging every sense of those unfortunate enough to be present and witness the attack. As the sun slowly rose in the east the next day, the fighting still raged.

"Southwesterly's air strikes on Washington – and the White House in particular – have been successful," a soldier reported to David and his counterparts from Northeasterly. "We have unverified reports that President King is fleeing but has met resistance from PA. Northeasterly troops have been diverted from the Mall."

"Thank you, Major." David said before turning to the Northeasterlians. "Seems to me that the United States just might be crumbling."

"Definitely teetering and about to fall," the senator from Northeasterly agreed.

With the Battle of Pennsylvania seemingly well under control, David and the Northeasterly team boarded a waiting helicopter and headed home.

"Guess we weren't really needed in Baltimore," David said.

"I suspect we served our purpose," the secretary of development disagreed. "King's people were tracking our movements; particularly yours."

Turning toward her and rolling his eyes at yet another comment of this kind, David said, "By the way, I'm kind of embarrassed at this point, but – I still don't know your names."

"Don't worry about that. With all that has been going on and happening so fast, the omission of formal introductions is unimportant. We're the Harcastles — I'm Ben and this is my wife, June."

"David Evans," he said and shook hands with each of them.

"That we know," June Harcastle stated. "You've been all over the Internet."

Arriving at the capitol and disembarking, the three were met by Fox and a person who identified himself as Marcus Marovitch of Southwesterly.

After a debriefing, the Harcastles broached another topic they wished to discuss. "Now that this battle appears to be won, we've been instructed to take one more try to get PA to join Northeasterly."

"I'm not sure whether this information will influence your decision," Marovitch spoke up, "but I feel I should tell you that our intelligence suggests that a number of central states are just waiting for this conflict to be over before announcing the formation of a new Midwesterly."

"So," Ben Harcastle stated the obvious, "the Independent Nation of Pennsylvania could end up standing alone. You don't want to put PA at a disadvantage," he continued, "by trying to survive separately with so much of the former United States being divvied up three ways."

Fox paused and looked across at David. Some sort of communication seemed to pass between them before he then stated, "Thanks anyway, but I think we have to try to finish what we started the way we started it and see where we land. The U.S. got too big," Fox concluded. "While that once offered a certain advantage to the economy and business, the scale of the country outgrew any human touch and is now too big to be the least bit personal and flexible." Just then, a call came through, and Fox excused himself to take it. After several moments, he returned to the room and announced, "King has fled the continent and appears to be heading to Eastern Europe. According to witnesses, U.S. troops are leaving their positions. The country appears to have crumbled and is now ours."

Marovitch and the Harcastles departed amicably. With the visitors gone, David said, "I believe you made the right decision."

"I hope so," Fox said softly, "though I suspect we've not heard the end of this."

"King's really gone?"

"Took his family, all his money, and headed out. We won't have to deal with him again," Fox said. Preparing to move on to his next task, he stopped long enough to say, "David, thanks for your help. I'd like to stay longer, but I better go brief my press secretary and communications' staff," he said with a smile. "She can be tough!"

David smiled and stated. "I'm heading back to Penndelom."

"Figured as much," the Governor acknowledged, "but I will ask that you return in a couple of days so we can regroup. I'll be suggesting that Jen come back for a bit, too."

About halfway home, David remembered to turn on his phone. As he flipped through channels to find the news, he came across Fox's press conference. He was telling his constituents about the fall of the United States, the desertion of King, and the heroic Battle of Pennsylvania that had been waged. He credited Northeasterly's involvement as being the deciding factor and extensively thanked David Evans for his successful diplomatic mission that made that possible.

The world was looking just a little bit different to David as the helicopter landed in Penndelom. The town was a little less dirty, a little less gray, and was a little warmer than usual for mid-March. So many changes had occurred in such short time.

Looking up at the clear, star-lit night as he crossed the tarmac, he felt energized to be part of something big. David was met by Jen and a fairly large group of supporters from Penndelom who greeted him like a long-lost hero. After he waded through all the backslapping, handshaking, and well wishes, he leaned over and whispered to Jen, "Let's go home."

Back inside their own apartment, greeted by an excited, tail-wagging cocker spaniel, Jen took David in her arms and said, "I have some bad news. I didn't want to tell you back in that crowd, but — John is missing in action. They called because he listed you as his contact person.

Missing, he thought. Not dead. Missing. There's hope.

Then aloud, "John is resourceful. Let's not count him out quite yet."

Looking Backward

Not so very long ago, the United States spanned a huge area from coast to coast and was ruled by a single, centralized government. From today's vantage point, such a map and political environment seem very hard to imagine. Surprisingly, the transformation happened quite quickly as the history below suggests.

The U.S. Teetered on the Brink. . . and Then Fell

While Pennsylvania was the first to separate from the United States, the decisions of California, Arizona, and Nevada to join forces in leaving the union and in creating a new country might well have been the most important acts of rebellion and certainly involved the greatest number of people and amount of real estate.

However, the price paid by these rebels was steep – with significant loss of life and damage to the landscape. Their resultant bitterness could not be overcome and would never leave. Decades into the future, the word King would be used as an ugly epithet spoken in anger.

Southwesterly

Unlike PA, the leaders of Southwesterly focused on building alliances that expanded their geographical boundaries. Due to the violence of the attacks on their land from the start, the people barely had the time or energy to react to events and lacked a clear vision of the kind of country they hoped to become. In Southwesterly, events and decisions were guided by instinct and natural inclination – such as a deep abiding optimism and rugged individualism – rather than plans. When approached by other states such as Oregon, Washington, Montana, etc. about the possibility of joining the alliance, a vague faith in gaining strength through numbers sealed the deal. Bigger was always better in their eyes.

On the day King shut down computer access to the western grid, people experienced a similar dislocation to that of Pennsylvanians. Since this new action had included a specially targeted attack on Silicon Valley – one of the primary centers for high technology – they lacked the resources to immediately start to work on getting a new system up and running as quickly as possible. Southwesterly had more immediate needs dealing with the damages of war. As a result, many of their solutions to help find a new normal were on the less technical side.

A strong, centralized government was never able to form in the west, though the informal relationships that did evolve were based on mutual need and desire and therefore were quite successful. Few people missed having the old-style political structure that was being replaced, and the leadership of Southwesterly was able to achieve the necessary consensus to move forward with new allies in defeating King.

Northeasterly

Elsewhere, the northeastern states – minus Pennsylvania – tried as much as possible to replicate the old U.S. government . . . but never believed that was their intention.   They managed to get some technology in place by paying premium ransom fees to hackers who stole enough programs and files to get a pirated system up and running. While far from perfect, this solution allowed the financial and information services industries to continue to dominate the culture.

While the unstated goal of Northeasterly was to maintain sameness, a surprising number of citizens took the opportunity to migrate to other neighboring regions that still had open-border policies.

Midwesterly

The Midwest was not such a place. Instead, that society stayed totally closed off from the rest and largely remained a mystery to those outside that immediate area. Conservative by nature and beliefs learned early at home, the new government was shaped around those ideals as well as an agricultural heritage shortly after the U.S. fell. According to the few people who chose to – or were allowed to – leave, the focus of those in charge was government control, not individual rights.

The World Had Realigned Overnight.

The United States – a mere shadow of its former self – became history with more of a whimper than a bang. Since four new jurisdictions had evolved – Southwesterly, Northeasterly, Midwesterly, and Pennsylvania – most former citizens slipped easily and comfortably into one of those new entities. Although quite a few states had not yet aligned themselves with one of the new nations, all of them gradually would within a few short years. An individual who never did fit into this newly re-shaped world was ex-President King. Having been commander-in-chief presiding over the fall of an empire, he took his riches and tried – but failed – to settle into several different places before ultimately landing in Monaco. He worked at projecting the image of someone thoroughly enjoying the good life, though he clearly appeared troubled about the perception future generations would have of him.

In those early stages of development, the ultimate shape of the new jurisdictions had yet to be determined, but a sense of optimism swept the land from coast to coast as people finally realized just how oppressed they had become.

Fireworks – End of an Era . . . and Start of Another

Before the great secession, people went about their daily lives – getting up, going to work, heading home to have dinner, and relaxing before going to bed; then, they repeated the same cycle. After the revolution, people went about their daily lives – getting up, going to work, heading home to have dinner, and relaxing before going to bed; then, they repeated the cycle.

Life was much the same on a certain level yet was fundamentally different.

Most folks now had a spring in their steps and started each day with a sense of hope that the next 24 hours would be better than the last.

Back in Penndelom, the citizens took pride in their actions in the past year and – right or wrong – took credit for all the subsequent events that led to the fall of one nation and the birth of several others. Specifically, they felt they had made a difference.

Summer in Penndelom always meant warm days and cool nights and kids playing baseball down by the little league field. Families cooked supper on grills and ate outside followed by slow walks through town to enjoy the sights and sounds of summer. Stopping at the center city bandstand to listen to a symphony of insects and watching fire flies light the sky, everyone – from older couples to teenagers – took advantage of the weather, the setting, and the opportunity to get to know each other better.

While the hardscape of the city had not yet changed much – tall glass buildings still dominated a concrete footprint lit by bright mercury streetlights – the place seemed somehow different, being warmer and more friendly than before.

That summer, Jen and David each settled into their new jobs and responsibilities. Although they split their time between Harrisburg and Penndelom – with their hectic roles and travel schedules consuming much of their time, energy, and attention – both were adapting to their very different routines as well as life together.

David, previously a virtual hermit, was thrust into a much more visible role than was natural or comfortable for him. He relied heavily upon Jen to help him navigate this new world. He had, in fact, begun to perceive himself somewhat differently and more positively because of his relationship with her. Their strengths and weaknesses – their similarities and differences – merged to create new versions of themselves. They were transformed into a couple following a single path forward into the future, where two paths previously existed.

Jen, for her part, seemed to take a much more deliberate approach to life than before, recognizing that her actions now affected two people and in a much more public way.

To them, Penndelom represented home – a safe place to be themselves, a slower-paced world that allowed them to get to know and explore each other better and in a leisurely way. Nevertheless, the town was changing, at least partly, to adapt to the new Independent Nation of Pennsylvania. Since the physical landscape was the same, a casual observer could be easily deceived into thinking that the transformation of the world had passed them by.

However, such was not the case. While you could still safely walk your dog late at night – which Jen and David often did – long lines at grocery stores betrayed production and supply chain issues. Car and truck traffic was reduced due to gasoline and electric charging station shortages, and police cars continually patrolled the streets for fear of post-insurrection terrorist activity.

Unlike the past, lit TV screens could be seen through very few living room windows because sources of packaged entertainment were limited in a society with more pressing priorities. As a result, more people sat on front porches late into the night, calling across to neighbors as children played outside at least into the early evening.

In other words, the world – like Jen and David – was also in the process of finding and defining a new self – though with a happier, more hopeful sense of optimism, despite being totally overwhelmed.

Back home for the 4th of July – now an historical footnote rather than a celebration – Jen and David laid quietly in bed, enjoying a moment of comfortable companionship.

On this particular night, almost all of Penndelom seemed to be out in the street and looking skyward – anticipating the start of fireworks.

Hearing loud voices outside their open widow, Jen leaned up on one elbow to better look at David when asking,

"Do you think much about the future?"

"Really been too busy to give that much thought."

She smiled and said, "I hear you, but I really can't stop wondering – What's next?"

Part II

Evolution – The Dawn of a New Day

Looking Backward

*The United States had been huge geographically as well as culturally diverse –
a system bound together by an exceptionally strong centralized bureaucracy.
In many ways, the resulting single government made no sense, which may have
ultimately led to the collapse over time. On the other hand, the United States
did manage a multi-century run, while the new nations experienced early
growing pains. During those first few tumultuous years of existence, most of
their time and efforts were devoted to figuring out who they were and the way
their countries would be governed.*

Just a Short Time Later . . .

*Two years after the six-month timeframe that changed the world – or at
least the boundaries of the United States of America – the four new upstart
nations that rose from the rubble of the fallen empire were still very much in
the process of taking shape. During those earliest days, the new governments
of Northeasterly, Midwesterly, Southwesterly, and Pennsylvania seemed to
reflect the nature of the people, the dominant activities of the area, and the
geography.*

*For example, Midwesterly was comprised of the former central
"breadbasket" states that generated much of the agribusiness of the U.S. While
the identities of the individual jurisdictions gradually disappeared and the
distinctions between Kansas and Nebraska, for instance, no longer mattered,
farming still ruled the midwestern portion of the continent, and the
government that was put into place was both conservative and libertarian.*

*Conversely, Northeasterly remained devoted to finance and information
service. Although this nation was initially structured to reflect the principles
of republicanism – an oligarchy gradually evolved.*

*Southwesterly probably had the purest form of a democracy and the most
diverse economy. However, some of the North Central region that elected to*

join the new union, such as Montana, probably fit less neatly than the western states that formed the core.

PA's experiment might have been the most radical. The head of state – Fred Fox, former Governor of the state of Pennsylvania – imagined a structure loosely resembling the organization of a business. Once he was elected CEO, together with other department chiefs of specific disciplines – known as the members of the "C-Suite" – he worked to put a system into place that was a flexible adaptation of the original.

During those early days when these new governments were still evolving, these countries – not yet in the habit of nationalism – started with open borders and free-trade policies, perhaps recognizing that everyone had friends and family scattered across the nations with almost no one in a position yet to actually choose their country based on personal preference. By allowing free movement and trade, the political structure encouraged people to forget a huge change had occurred, enabling them to largely continue their old daily lives. After a couple of years had passed, an oft speculated return to isolationism and an era of decline and regression had not yet materialized.

Closing Borders

In two days, her cousin Flora was getting married, and Jen was part of the wedding party. As a result, she and David were leaving now for upstate New York.

Although Jen had spoken with her retired parents regularly during the fall of the U.S., and despite the fact that they had regularly read her articles about events in the newspaper, she had not visited them in months. Consequently, she was looking forward to seeing them at the wedding.

Normally, the trip would be considered a relatively short jaunt of just a few hours from Northeast PA. However, times had changed. Her cousin Flora's town was now part of a different country.

Flora was not political. As a result, she viewed this change as a personal inconvenience and not much more.

"You know," David said to Jen as she finished getting ready to go, "Flora's lucky that Pennsylvania and Northeasterly currently maintain an open border policy. The way discussions are going, that might not continue to be the case soon."

"That could prove difficult. While my parents fortunately live in PA, I've got lots of aunts, uncles, and cousins scattered across the old United States who are now spread throughout four different countries."

"My guess," David said, "is that your situation will not be all that uncommon. Although our future might not be as bad as East and West Germany in the past, we all are going to have to get used to dealing with barriers to easy interaction." Glancing at his watch, he then asked, "Are you just about ready to go?"

"Just about," she said. "The car packed?"

"Hours ago."

"Not exactly looking forward to the next several days, are you?" she asked.

"Not true and not fair," he complained. "I'm anxious to meet your immediate family – your parents and sisters. It's just the other 300 people that seems a bit overwhelming."

"250."

"My mistake."

"How did I ever end up with such an introvert?"

"Just lucky I guess."

As it was currently midsummer, Jen and David enjoyed the drive to the wedding on a bright sunny day with temperatures in the mid-80's. The rural landscape was an especially vivid green reminiscent of images of Ireland.

Home to several universities, Hamilton was a classic rural college town. Jen's cousin landed here first as a student and then as a graduate teaching assistant.

Following the GPS's directions, they were told to turn left onto a dirt road that led to a large barn about a half mile later where they were told by a very slightly mechanical voice, "You have arrived at your destination."

Seeing her cousin, Jen waved and hollered, "We at the right place?"

"You got the address from the invitation, right? Our reception is at this barn; the church and house are up the road."

Jen got out of the car as her cousin approached and gave her a hug. "We're not the first, are we?"

"Hardly. Your parents got to town yesterday, and both of your sisters arrived this morning."

"And who, might I ask, is your chauffer?"

"David, come say hello to Flora."

"Flora, I'd like you to meet my boyfriend, David Evans." Jen always flinched at the word boyfriend, a term that made their relationship seem very teenaged.

"Do I recognize you?" Flora gave him a hug. "Your face looks awfully familiar."

"I suspect I just have one of those faces," David answered, though Jen quickly countered, "You've probably seen his picture on the Internet and in the media. He's in a constant state of denial about being recognizable. Besides, he now holds a job with Fred Fox's new government, and we all know how well publicized each of his new appointments has been."

"Yep," Flora agreed. "That could certainly be the reason."

"Or perhaps I really do just have one of those average-looks-like-everybody-kinds-of-faces," David countered.

David ascended to the position of Deputy CEO — or second-in-command — when Ron Rose was killed. This role – like all others within the new nation – was ill-defined and came without a job description. Ron Rose never had a chance to put his stamp on the position, so David had no precedents to guide him. Therefore, he basically did any tasks that Fox requested and otherwise just acted when some intervention felt right.

Fox also seemed to be figuring things out as he went but clearly appeared to want David more and more involved. He kept referring to their executive partnership – the "executive" label coming from the branch of government they represented, not some C-Suite status consciousness.

That said, David felt as though his major accomplishment to date had been to warm his seat at endless meetings that kept him going back to Harrisburg. More recently, Fox seemed to have David slated to take a more active part in current discussions about closing the borders of Pennsylvania without alienating their larger new neighbors or having them perceive this decision as an act of hostility.

David had developed several key relationships a few years back. He felt comfortable approaching them in an informal way but was not sure he totally understood or agreed with Fox's desire to close the border.

While he knew the intent and goal was to promote self-sufficiency and discourage just looking to other markets to obtain needed goods they could not produce themselves, he also feared that isolationism might have a negative impact upon the sharing of information, scientific breakthroughs, and cultural exchanges. History clearly reflected that such a political posture presented many dangers.

Aside from the possible economic impact, David knew Fox felt very uncertain about the potential for wholesale immigration to – or emigration from – PA. While he really couldn't predict whether either of these trends would occur, he foresaw dangers in both.

Furthermore, David did wonder whether their new neighboring nations would decide to retaliate and do likewise . . . and wondered whether Pennsylvania was ready for the challenge of going forward alone.

Nevertheless, David liked Fox and trusted his instincts. So, he was inclined to give him the benefit of the doubt in such matters until proven wrong.

David knew he'd be arranging a meeting with his contacts from Northeasterly as soon as the wedding was over and he and Jen were back in Penndelom.

He wasn't exactly looking forward to those events and was once again quick to question whether he was really cut out to deal with the role of diplomat that he was increasingly asked to play.

Dressed for the wedding rehearsal, again reminded just how beautiful Jen was and how fortunate he was to have found her or – more accurately – that she had found him, David was about to be introduced to her parents, who had invited them to their room for a meet-and-greet drink before joining the wedding party.

David knew Jen was very close to her family and had heard enough stories to have a few preconceived notions about them. He expected her father to be fairly outgoing, her mother somewhat reserved, and both of them very polished and well spoken.

They did not disappoint.

"So, we finally get to meet the hero of the Internet," Jen's father teased.

"I told you not to bring that up!" she implored.

"Which is exactly the reason he did," her mother countered. "Very pleased to meet you, David; don't mind Jenny's father. He thinks he's being funny."

"Pleased to meet you both," David said.

"Beautiful day; hope tomorrow's as nice for the wedding," Jen's mother added. "Still can't believe Flora's old enough to be getting married."

"What can I get you to drink?" Jen's father asked. "Champagne? Bit early, but today's a special occasion."

"Sure."

"So, David," her father continued, "what's new in Harrisburg, and what is Fred Fox up to these days?"

David knew from Jen that her dad and Fred Fox had met years ago over a deal involving his manufacturing plant. He also knew that he was basically a supporter of Fox and had voted for secession. However, Jen never acknowledged the relationship to Fox, not wanting to risk any appearance of conflict of interest.

"I think he's just trying to take each day as it comes, to figure out the structures and systems needed to keep the state – I mean country – up and running."

"I've heard some rumblings about PA closing borders," her dad said. "Any truth to that?"

"No more politics," Jen's mother warned.

Jen, trying to avoid intervening, raised her glass in a toast, "To Flora," glancing in David's direction and catching his eye, which seemed to be smiling. She then added, "And to new beginnings."

During the next half hour, both Jen and David tried to explain their jobs to her father, which they still only partially understood themselves, particularly David's. He also heard Jen recounting some of the details of their first meeting and early days as a couple. Now together two years, Jen had many opportunities to tell their story, so she had developed a fairly condensed, polished version that she could recount on demand in just a few minutes – a skill sure to come in handy as she met various relatives during the course of the wedding celebration.

Jen, David, and her parents made their way from their hotel room to the wedding rehearsal at the church. Using the hotel shuttle, they were able to enjoy the late afternoon warmth and the sights of the rural countryside connecting the small towns.

Arriving at the destination – a small wooden church suitable for a Norman Rockwell painting – the four of them entered and were introduced to the other members of the wedding party.

Jen's parents were described as an aunt and uncle who were like a second mother and father, so their participation in the practice run was honorary. Jenny was referred to as the sister the bride never had. David was just, "Jenny's new friend."

When Flora was about to introduce the best man, Alan Hall, he interrupted her to say, "I'm actually aware of who David Evans is. I work for Ben and June Harcastle as their assistant. When they heard I was attending a wedding, with Jen and David on hand, they wanted me to be sure to pass along their regards. I also have a message . . . but that can wait.

"Sounds good," David responded. "I'm an admirer of your employers."

As the bridal party gathered at the front of the church to receive their instructions, David took a seat among the audience and watched. Once done, everyone was to adjourn to the home of the bride's parents for a post-rehearsal barbeque.

The night was warm and clear. After dinner, everyone was mingling, and the best man, Alan Hall, approached Jen and David.

Sorry to bother you, but I've been asked by Ben and June to see whether a meeting might be arranged in a few days. "Ironic," David responded. "That was the item at the top of my 'to do' list upon getting back. Any idea what they want to discuss?"

"The closing of borders."

"Of course. That was my subject as well. How does three days from now sound? I can meet them in Boston."

"Perfect . . . but I'll just need to quickly confirm the exact time."

"I'd expect no less."

"Do me a favor and go dance with my mother. My father's not a dancer."

"And I am?"

"She's been sitting by herself most of the night."

"The music just started a little while ago," he stated, then saw the disappointed look on her face, and continued, "but I will dutifully do as you ask."

"Thank you," Jen said, but he was already halfway to the other side of the ballroom.

Dancing to an old, slow, 50's tune, David started to make some small talk, but Jen's mother interrupted, "You can tell a lot about a relationship by the way couples react to small requests. When you see evidence of automatic consideration and small kindnesses, you know the couple's bonds are very strong. I figure Jenny sent you over to dance with me and you did so willingly. That's the kind of interaction I'm talking about. As long as you keep that up, you will be okay."

"I'm crazy about your daughter."

"I can tell. I can also see the feeling is mutual. She's never seemed happier or more content."

"I certainly hope so."

"How old are you, David?"

"Just turned 36. About an 11-year difference in age but it feels like less."

"That wasn't what I was questioning. Just trying to get a sense of whether you are ready to settle down."

"I came wired that way, even as a kid."

"That's not the sense I got from reading about you in the news."

"That person is not me. He's an invention of the media, and I don't mean that critically. I think they do a good job – especially your daughter. When you are a reporter describing certain actions and results without the time and space to disclose the entire context, you can't help but end up with a bit of a caricature that depends upon the readers' imaginations to fill in unspoken details."

"You and Jenny do seem to be well matched. Just remember to stay attentive to the small kindnesses. That will ensure your relationship stays strong."

As the post-rehearsal party wound down, David and Jen said goodnight to her parents and Flora before heading back to their hotel. They were tired. Between the travel and having to be "on" for countless people – many of them new acquaintances – they were ready for bed and an early night.

Tomorrow, David would be meeting Jen's sisters, as well as a couple of hundred others. Lots of good reasons to need some rest.

Waking early, they grabbed some breakfast at the hotel before Jen went to discharge her wedding party duties. Her sisters were either older or younger than the bride, so only Jen was participating in the wedding party.

David, walking the grounds of the hotel, was enjoying the cooler morning and the scenery when he heard someone calling out his name.

The best man, who worked for the Harcastles.

"You're up early. Shouldn't you be doing best man stuff now?" David asked, only half in jest – not really wanting to have his reveries interrupted.

"Best men don't really have many duties. Just have to be sure not to screw up the rings."

"Nice morning."

"So, you're Jenny's . . ."

"Yep. I'm Jenny's . . ." David decided to spare him the challenge of coming up with the right word.

"How do you know the Harcastles?"

"I'm sure they told you the story as part of the process of giving you this assignment," David responded.

"They did. Just wanted to hear your version."

"I'm sure mine is exactly the same as theirs," David smiled, "whatever that might be."

"I spoke with them last night," Alan got down to business. "The plan for you to meet them in three days in Boston is perfect. Consider the arrangements confirmed. I was also instructed to tell you that they look forward to seeing you again."

David thanked him for the quick work and the message. He then started to say, "I better get going," when the best man said, "Time for me to go check on the whereabouts of those rings, so I don't mess up my small part."

The ceremony was lovely and also quite quick. Once the couple exchanged their vows, kissed, and headed back out of the church, the wedding party left by the side door to meet for the wedding photos.

About an hour and a half later, David and Jen were headed to the reception.

"Nicely done," Jen said. "They streamlined every activity without compromising the quality or significance of the moment."

"Agreed," David said. "One of these days, we'll have to talk about doing that ourselves."

Jen smiled but said nothing – not sure the degree to which he was being serious.

David and Jen were seated at a table with her sisters, though her parents were at a different place with her aunts and uncles. The older sister, Olivia, said, "I've looked forward to meeting the man who managed to take my kid sister off the market and out of circulation."

"Odd way of introducing yourself, Liv," Jen remarked.

"So, you're the Internet guy," Jen's younger sister, Samantha, stated.

"Sam!"

"Ooops. Wasn't supposed to bring that up, though clearly that's the elephant in the room. How'd you manage to get all of that publicity?"

"Just seems to seek out those of us who want no part of that."

"I've got to go back up front," Jen said, "but I promise these two will behave themselves, right girls?"

"Who us?" Liv asked, pretending to be the picture of innocence.

"I'll keep an eye on them," Sam offered with a wink.

"I'll be back," Jen reminded them. "Liv, introduce David to the others at the table."

After David met the five other cousins seated at their eight-person round, Liv explained, "I really am very pleased to meet you."

"Likewise."

"I've been thinking about moving to Albany and applying for citizenship with Northeasterly, any reason not to consider that?"

"Possibility of a closed border," David answered. "Seems more and more likely every day, and you could end up getting cut off from the rest of your immediate family."

"Why, Liv?" Sam demanded.

"The guy I've been seeing. His family is from New York."

"You wouldn't!" Sam seemed to be trying to convince herself.

"Maybe," Liz said as she took another sip of wine.

As they were dancing, David said, "So, looks like I'm headed to Boston on Wednesday. Care to come?"

"Wish I could," Jen responded, "but I'm in the middle of a press release I need to finish about the new government."

"Anything interesting?"

"Not really, though I understand the center of power is now mostly with the Deputy CEO."

"Ha. Ha."

"Seriously, I suspect the meeting with the folks from Northeasterly will be important."

"You think?" David countered. "My guess is they've already made up their minds, and I'm being used as a live-and-in-person messenger boy, which is just fine by me. However, nothing will be determined by this trip. If PA closed the borders, they are just using me to tell Fox exactly what to expect from Northeasterly."

Grabbing David's arm and simulating having this introvert spin her around, Jen smiled at him and said, "Now that's the spirit!" – which prompted him to drop her into a very small dip as they enjoyed the rest of the reception party.

The trip back from the wedding was pleasant, but the subsequent trip to Boston came way too soon afterwards. While David had been instructed by Fred Fox to use a helicopter, David wanted to arrive with less fanfare and had himself dropped off outside the city.

After a short drive and check in at the hotel, David took a taxi to the meeting. Upon arriving, Alan Hall, from the wedding – now acting in his official capacity as an aid – greeted him, "The Harcastles are waiting for you in their suite. I'll take you."

"Thanks. Enjoy the wedding?"

"Yup, and I didn't mess up the rings."

"Well done."

"David, so good to see you again," said June Harcastle.

"The pleasure is all mine,"

"I understand the wedding was beautiful. Alan – our aid – is a very old friend of the groom."

"He acquitted himself well and carried out his duties flawlessly."

"Certainly, the circumstances of this meeting are a lot more pleasant than the last one," stated Ben.

"Yes," David agreed, "though we were far from the actual fighting, the war – the battle – was nearby."

"We understand you were hoping to speak with us, too," June shifted the topic to the business at hand.

"Yes. I've been asked to let you know that Pennsylvania is considering closing its border. As our nearest neighbor, we didn't want to surprise you or leave you wondering about our motives, which have nothing to do with you. Our Chief, Fred Fox, believes the long-term best interests of our people will be served by forcing them to be self-reliant in every possible way. As long as the border remains open and every need can be addressed in a nearby country, he doesn't think self-sufficiency will happen. The decision is no reflection upon our relationship with you, which we hope can remain very strong and amicable even after the fact."

"David," Ben Harcastle said, "we happen to believe Fred is misreading the situation. We don't think your citizens will accept the decision and obediently change their ways. Frankly, we see protests occurring and a general public outcry to join the union of Northeasterly rather than endure the hardship of learning new ways."

"You underestimate us," David started to say when June interrupted, "Well, we will soon learn who is right. David, our government has decided to be proactive. Rather than wait for you to close your border, our bosses – convinced they can predict the ultimate outcome – have decided to close Northeasterly's border first."

Taking a moment to absorb this unexpected turn, David smiled and asked, "So, is the decision already made – or is your next step going to be an offer to keep this from happening by doing 'something' that you want done."

"Reasonable question, but no, the decision has been made. In the interest of continuing our positive relationship, we wanted to provide advance warning. Frankly, the general feeling is that no other step but closing the border will be needed to have PA eventually come to us asking to become part of our union, which you know has long been our goal."

"Well, I will let Fred know."

"Hopefully, our next meeting will be under more favorable circumstances."

"You mean as part of the same team?"

"Exactly."

"I wouldn't count on that."

"David, off the record. Please tell Fred to be very careful. We have some real militant parties that want to take Pennsylvania back, doing whatever might be necessary. I believe these people are dangerous in general but to Fred in particular. Please warn him.

As usual, David wished Fred Fox had been able to attend this meeting as well. Frankly, David always felt a bit over-matched with the Harcastles, and he felt Fred would be better equipped, having the experience, training, and insight to better know whether the couple was being totally straightforward or was laying some groundwork of their own that David could not see.

Though the Harcastles had always been very upfront with David and had proven to be very honest and forthright, David understood that they, too, had a job to do.

Naturally, this line of thinking got him wishing he'd never agreed to take this or any other job in the new government. Instead, he longed for the days when work just meant being the local A/V guy.

Daily Herald OpED

The Displaced
by Dr. Garfield Payne – Professor
Political Science
Penndelom Community College

With geopolitical change occurring across North America, many people have become displaced. Like everyone else, I've heard the stories. However, this matter also has a much more personal and immediate meaning for me.

I am a long-term resident of Pennsylvania – born and raised in the central part of the state. I come from a small family and have one brother. After getting his degree from Penn State, he took a job in Rhode Island, which is now part of a separate country called Northeasterly. His son grew up in Providence and went to Brown but ended up taking a job very close to me. My niece, his daughter, took a position in California and morphed into a citizen of Southwesterly. My son, an only child, was a graduate student and instructor at Notre Dame at the time of the great political upheaval, so he was automatically granted citizenship in Midwesterly.

Although immediate relocation back to Pennsylvania has certainly been an option for all my family during the earliest months of the transformation, none of the Paynes have been in a position to abandon their current lives and start anew. Such dislocation has been impractical, and these new countries have been unwilling to offer dual citizenship, though they did – at least initially – allow free travel back and forth across borders.

Needless to say, I now take this matter very personally. In fact, I've pretty much decided my wife and I may have to be the ones to move to stay close to our son. Frankly, our established careers are coming to a close in just a few years, so we see no immediate alternative to making this sacrifice.

My situation is not unique.

Furthermore, I want to point out that the displaced also includes both employees and companies. Particularly among larger regional and national entities, many workers are physically located in areas now split into a different country than the home office. Suddenly, long-term staff assigned to satellite locations in one of the new jurisdictions have found themselves needing special temporary work permits — when they could get them — or new jobs. Similarly, corporations with multiple offices must now treat portions of their operations as international, including payment of new taxes, tariffs, and penalties imposed by the start-up governments.

The other category of often overlooked displaced people includes some individuals who have remained in the same location but simply cannot any longer recognize this new world as their own — leaving them feeling like aliens in their homelands. This group, by far the largest, probably faces the most difficult future challenges because they cannot solve their problem by simply relocating.

So, where does this situation leave us? What is the solution I need to offer in writing this editorial?

Since I do not believe that a return to the old ways is either an option or desirable, I suppose I am looking to a fourth faction for my answer. These people are the ones who initially felt like intruders in their own country but have grown much more attuned over time to the altered landscape. This group, which includes citizens from each of the new countries, are the ones who have learned over time to feel as though they'd found their homes and are the ones who give me hope.

Meanwhile, I remain separated from my immediate family. So, I will end this article with a plea for every country to reconsider the decision to close their borders and eliminate free trade. In doing so, I believe they will be giving more and more of their citizens, like me, a chance to join the fourth group by allowing them the freedom to remain close to their families.

While the creation of new governments capable of delivering essential services must certainly be a main preoccupation of those in charge, dealing with the displaced will, to a large degree, determine the ultimate success or failure of this brave new world.

John, The MIA

The recent conflict with the United States left many casualties.

David's life-long friend, John O'Hara, was a member of the National Guard who was called to active duty. His platoon was sent to Philadelphia at the height of the conflict, and he was reported missing in action not long afterwards.

Fortunately, John was mostly a victim of confusion. After doing his part in Philly, John was part of a team that set out for Camp David, Maryland – a possible landing spot of then President King. Unfortunately, he and his team never arrived. The trucks handling the transport were hit by an artillery attack that disabled all but one or two of the vehicles carrying the troops, and many lives were lost in the destruction.

With only a dozen men left – clearly not enough to do much good at Camp David – John and the other survivors set out for Harrisburg, figuring they'd cross paths with some friendlies and could join them.

They were in the process of carrying out this plan when the first soldiers they met up with were from Southwesterly. Nevertheless, John and his group accompanied them as they traveled south toward Washington D.C. While they were not part of the PA regiment, Southwesterly was at least an ally who had sprung to the defense of

Pennsylvania. As a result, John felt okay about traveling with them – recognizing the advantage of strength in numbers. He had felt very vulnerable when the dozen of them had been heading north alone.

After a day on the road, the soldiers had just arrived at the outskirts of D.C. when another attack by King's forces disrupted the convoy.

John's transport was again hit, though this time he was not so lucky. Bleeding from some shrapnel in his leg, he felt a searing pain, but knew, unlike many others, that he was fortunate to be alive.

While the medics from Southwesterly performed an efficient extraction, John idly wondered through the morphine whether he might lose his leg, and this troubling thought was the last one he had before he passed out and was loaded onto a helicopter heading for the west coast.

John was in the hospital for weeks, but the doctors managed to save his leg. Many months of rehabilitation followed, and he did all that was required to regain his strength and mobility. He also fell in love with his physical therapist Joanna.

While she liked John very much, she realized that patients often grew attached to their medical team, so she initially kept her guard up and kept her distance.

Gradually, John seemed to convince her that he was feeling far more than a simple case of transference.

While she repeatedly asked John who she might contact for him, he had decided he wanted to fully recover before getting back in touch with his old world and life. He knew David and Jen would be quick to come help, but he also knew that the two of them were busy building a life and, in fact, a country and didn't need the baggage of a convalescent. He did miss his dog, who would have been great company right now. However, he knew the pup was in good hands.

Besides, John was quite taken with Joanna and could see himself settling down in this part of the world. Though he had never before traveled beyond Ohio, he found a lot to like about the west. He felt a certain attraction to the ruggedness of the Sierra Nevada mountains, which were higher, younger, and rougher than those on the east coast. They made their presence known and felt.

He also liked the spaciousness – enjoyed having more distance between clusters of civilization with fewer towns and cities crammed into the available land.

Perhaps most of all, he sensed a real difference in the people he met – almost everyone seemed to have a fundamentally optimistic outlook on life, perhaps an outgrowth of a closer rapport with nature . . . or maybe just a sense that they had more control over their destiny in a part of the country that was younger and, therefore, had a shorter history of mistakes to overcome.

Southwesterly, as a whole, reflected many of the qualities of the citizenry, and John found himself drawn to a country that seemed to look toward the future with confidence and faith in a better world ahead.

Yes, John could see himself fitting into this landscape but felt he needed Joanna to serve as his guide and had to convince her to assume that role.

As time passed, John and Joanna became a couple, moved in together, and were expecting a child. Although the better part of two years had been required, John was almost fully recovered – at least as recovered as he would ever get.

About six months ago, he reached a new plateau in this process and began working as a teacher – a profession that seemed to suit him.

Over the past few days, John had felt a strong compulsion to share his news and had finally decided to reach out to David and Jen.

When he told Joanna about his decision and described the people he intended to call, she immediately said, "You don't mean *the* David Evans, do you?"

"Well, I don't know. He's definitely 'a' David Evans. Whether or not he's the same as your David Evans remains to be seen."

"Quite the Internet celebrity a few years back during the war. Now, a pretty big wig in PA's new government. That David Evans?"

"Yep. That's the one."

"And that would mean that the Jen you are talking about is Fred Fox's press secretary."

"You keep up with the news. Yes. I guess so."

"And . . . were you . . .are you . . .an important person?"

"Me?" John laughed. "Hell no . . . and they weren't either when I knew them."

"Why wait so long to get in touch?"

"I needed to get fixed, both physically and mentally, and didn't want to disrupt their lives. They are good people. Seeing them now, I believe is the right decision. Besides, I miss my dog!"

"Are you planning to fly back east?"

"No. I'll just call. My life is here now. I don't belong to their world but would like them to be a part of our lives. I figure we can ask David – as my oldest and best friend – to be the godfather of our child.

After so much time had passed, John felt awkward about calling David and just showing up in his life again without explanation. So, he procrastinated. He poured himself a cup of coffee. He used the bathroom. He paced around the room and mentally pictured the three of them on the last day before he went away. Still not knowing exactly what he was going to say to his oldest friend but anxious to renew the connection, he dialed the number and waited through four rings until he heard the phone picked up and said, "David?"

"Hello. Yes. This is David Evans."

"This is John."

Silence.

"David?"

"Whoever you are, this call better not be a practical joke," David's voice was infused with anger tinged with sadness. "I have not seen or heard from my friend John O'Hara in years.

"Two and a half to be exact. I can explain," John said defensively. "Do you have the time?"

"Of course," David answered and then added, "but this better be good."

"I'll get to my story, but first I need to know how my pup Fala is?"

Debriefing

Traveling back from Boston to Harrisburg, the day was bright and sunny with no turbulence, so David could sit back and enjoy the scenery.

"I've been asked to take you directly to Mr. Fox's office for a debriefing upon your arrival," the pilot stated.

"That's fine. Expected as much."

He tried to call Jen but kept getting a busy signal, so he left a brief message: "I expect you and I will be able to head back to Penndelom tonight. I can't wait to see you to tell you about an interesting phone call I received."

"David, welcome back," Fox said and then asked, "Good trip?"

"Just okay. I delivered your message but ran into an unexpected twist."

"Have a seat. What kind of twist?"

"Apparently," David explained, "Northeasterly had heard enough rumors about our plans to close our borders that they decided to take pre-emptive action. They have elected to close their borders first."

"Hmmmm," was Fox's response.

171

"No hard feelings, mind you," David was quick to qualify his remarks, "They just figure that acting first is the best way for them to come out ahead."

"So where does that leave us," Fox mused aloud.

"Well, we certainly gain nothing by doing nothing," David offered. "Seems like we have no choice but to move forward as previously discussed and close our borders anyway."

"I agree," Fox responded, "but I suspect this turn of events complicates matters a bit."

"How so?"

"We seem to have become the mean-spirited party that just acted out of revenge," Fox paused a moment, then clarified his comment. "Our decision no longer seems to be part of a carefully planned strategy to gain self-sufficiency. I had hoped to leverage opening the border against progress in meeting our goal and build some momentum and national pride. I don't think that is possible now."

"I see," David responded, "but I still think you might be able to link the action to your campaign, just a little less directly."

"Was that the only issue discussed?"

"Yes. The meeting was quite short. I do generally like and trust the Harcastles. I don't think they are just playing political games."

"Though they were just the messengers," Fox reminded him.

"I suspect they are a bit more than that," David countered. "Nothing specific to prove my point, but I actually believe they participate in policy discussions."

"How fast will this happen?" Fox probed further.

"Probably as we speak."

"Then, we better not delay in getting our message out. I'll have Jen draft the announcement for release tomorrow with an implementation target date one week from now. That will just barely give us time to get our systems and resources put into place along our borders."

"Can we really pull that off so fast?" David asked. "I'm guessing Northeasterly had all of those arrangements made before Ben and June spoke to us."

"No doubt. However, speed and flexibility are supposed to be key benefits of staying small and lean as an independent country," Fox reminded him.

"If you say so . . ."

"Thanks for taking care of the Northeasterly meetings, David. Good to have you back."

"Fred, I think I better give you one more heads up that the Harcastles seemed to make a point of telling me. Apparently, Northeasterly has a small but very active and vocal militant faction that is obsessed with the idea of absorbing Pennsylvania into their new country and who see you as a major obstacle. Probably nothing to be done about that, but you need to be armed with that knowledge, so you'll stay alert."

"I'll let the Harcastles know I appreciate that bit of intelligence."

"I'm working late, but you apparently already know the reason," Jen said.

"True. Your call: do we stay the night in Harrisburg or just wait and head back to Penndelom when you're ready?" David asked. "I'm okay either way."

"Let's try to stick to our plan to head back tonight. Once I get Fox's feedback, make any changes, and hear more about the schedule for tomorrow, "I'll have a better idea."

"Fine by me. Since we are going to be awhile, let me give you a preview of the news I have to tell you."

"Ooooh-kay," she said hesitantly.

"I got a call from John O'Hara. He's alive and well."

"Oh my God," she started to say, but David interrupted, "The rest can wait until later. He's good, but the story is long. I figure dangling this tickler will motivate you to write quickly."

Back in Penndelom

"So, is John planning to stay in Southwesterly, or will he eventually head home?" Jen asked.

"He sounded pretty entrenched. A couple of years is a long time, and he's already planted some pretty deep roots. New family. New career. Basically, a new life and one that's more complete than the one he left behind. What do you think?" David asked Jen rhetorically.

"I think him not contacting us till now is a little odd."

"He explained that, and his motives were pure."

"But Southwesterly," Jen said, "is *very* different. Does he really fit? Can he make that adjustment?"

"The life he knew in Pennsylvania is also gone," David replied. "He's adjusting regardless. In Southwesterly, he gets warmer temperatures, lots of open outdoor space, *and* a brand-new democracy that seems to be building around the old-fashioned idea of everyone having a voice. Town meetings. Majority rules. No large Political Action Committees with lots of money to buy votes, and no PACs should mean more honest and legitimate results."

"Sounds pretty good," Jen agreed. "I guess I'm convinced. When do we leave? I'm game but only on the condition that neither of us has an official public role."

"Deal," David said jokingly and then added, "Southwesterly may turn out to be the only one among us to do things right. I fear the folks in Midwesterly are going to end up making that an uncomfortably conservative place that constantly impinges upon people's rights and keeps getting more and more reactionary."

"And PA?" Jen asked.

"Very much a work in progress. Perhaps the most different approach, so it makes sense that more time would be needed."

With both of them lost in thought and the hour very late, Jen and David briefly sat in silence as the helicopter began its slow descent.

After thanking the pilot for taking the extra trip at 3:00 in the morning, they got into their car for the last leg of their journey home.

"How many times have we taken this trip?" Jen asked.

"Too many," David answered without hesitation. "At what point can we feel free to quit these jobs and live a more normal life?"

"I don't know," she answered seriously. "I think we are both expecting to reach some magic moment that has a sense of closure that tells us our work is done and we've given all that we had to offer. Then, we'd be ready."

"Unfortunately, that might never happen. Meanwhile, I can think of a hundred people who can do my job as well or better than I can," David stated, "though you've become pretty irreplaceable to Fox."

"Wrong on both counts," Jen responded as they arrived home.

Quite intentionally changing the subject, David said, "Did Liv also mention to you that she might move to Northeasterly and renounce her Pennsylvania citizenship?"

"Yes. She mentioned that, and I tried to discourage her."

"Me, too. Just bad timing with the border closings."

Two years into the process of reconstruction, the four new countries were just now having to face some very difficult questions that would have a huge impact upon people's future lives.

With the closure of the border between Pennsylvania and Northeasterly, various relatives who were scattered across the old United States, which covered most of the continent, were now going to have to choose between relocation and a possible loss of family ties due to the elimination off free movement.

Earlier that day, David had warned Fred Fox about this possible byproduct of any attempt to close borders. He had expressed the opinion that all four of the countries would likely follow suit and believed that many people would be forced to finally choose citizenship in the place that made the most sense rather than just accept the country where they happened to be when the war began and ended.

While he was unsure about the country Jen's sister would ultimately choose, he did know that the situation had them asking the same questions about themselves and their future.

David and Jen basically liked the life that seemed to be taking shape at home, and they'd started to resent duties that forced them to be away for any length of time.

Since seceding from the United States, most of the changes had been good ones from their vantage point: going from a large nation to a small one, from fast to slow, and from helpless to much more in control of their own destiny.

Pennsylvania still enjoyed the many services you got from a large country – without having to constantly report your whereabouts to a big, central computer system that controlled movement and access to everything.

In other words, life had assumed a comfortable routine. Jen and David each had a separate work area and spent most mornings on the computer. They ate lunch together and then went back to work – often involved in video conferences. They took turns making dinner and often cooked together. They shopped for groceries about once a week.

The country was now running very smoothly in providing the essentials needed for daily life. Fortunately, the financial infrastructure was restored very quickly, and the supply chain was unbroken, though PA relied very heavily upon neighboring countries for most products. That, of course, was Fox's major concern and the reason he was closing the border.

The circumstances in the other three countries were quite similar, though Northeasterly might have been the most reliant upon others and, therefore, the most vulnerable. Otherwise, life in those places seemed to move forward without major disruption – largely because of the amicable relationships with others.

Food and other necessities were available in sufficiently abundant quantities as well as luxury items. Unemployment was universally low in all four nations, and people were enjoying a period of relative peace and prosperity. Unfortunately, that seemed destined to end soon.

When PA closed the border, certainly light manufacturing would be missed elsewhere as some products became scarce, and distribution became more of an issue. In addition, doubt remained about whether or not Pennsylvania and the others could survive without the food produced in Midwesterly.

Any shortages were likely to produce anger and perhaps even violence.

In anticipation, Fox had funded lots of new agricultural initiatives. Whether they would succeed soon enough and well enough to make a difference remained to be seen.

Late one afternoon, Jen got the call to issue her press release about PA's decision to close the border, giving people and businesses just a week to prepare prior to implementation.

Since she had spent much of the day anticipating this moment, Jen was able to meet the late afternoon deadlines for getting the news included in evening broadcasts and early morning newspapers.

The text was actually quite short and flat in tone, dealing specifically with the facts about the "when" and the "how" this action would be taken rather than elaborating on the "why." On Fox's instruction, she had simply mentioned in passing that the decision was strictly an internal priority and not a thinly veiled threat or warning directed at other countries.

When all the necessary e-mails and text messages had been sent, Jen called Fox's assistant, Gretchen Moriority, to let her know.

"All done."

"Any contacts from the media yet?"

"No. The announcement just went out, which is the reason I'm calling you now. Wanted to provide a heads-up so you could screen calls."

"Thanks. Timely. The other lines on my phone are starting to light up."

"Mine, too," Jen responded. "Talk to you later."

With that, she started answering call after call for the next three hours. Journalists from all four countries had been notified and at least one person from the communications staff of each government had been contacted and were already back in touch with her.

As she'd stated in the press releases, little additional information was provided at this time because Fox planned to deliver a follow-up speech the next day. They figured the 24-hour time lapse between the two events – while short – would still give them an opportunity to gauge both public and press reactions to the news.

Thus far, Jen was confident she could tell Fox that Northeasterly's reaction had been the most extreme. Her contact from Southwesterly did not seem especially troubled and indicated that they would wait for the speech and might then have further questions. Her counterpart from Midwesterly didn't make a big deal of the news but did say, "Who does Fox think he is? Must have a pretty big ego; the decision reeks of self-importance."

Northeasterly was the most outspoken, which – as the closest neighbor – made sense. Proximity alone seemed to suggest greater inconvenience than that experienced by the others.

One after the other, Jen took the calls and basically repeated the same message – mostly dealing with other press secretaries and reporters. Due to the time difference, she was still getting questions from the west coast at 8:00 pm her time.

Tired and hungry, she saw David enter the room.

"You survive ok?" he asked.

"Barely."

"Ready to knock off for the day? First round of broadcast news is already over. Ended at 7:00 and seemed fine."

"Just fine?" Jen said.

"Very fine," David corrected himself with a smile. "Take a break."

"Not quite yet. I have a debriefing with Fox in ten minutes. After that, we can probably eat."

"Good luck. I'll make dinner."

"He'll want you on the call."

Sighing, he agreed, "You're probably right."

The session with Fox lasted about an hour. Jen recapped the calls she'd gotten and the comments she'd received as well as summarizing the reports from the various TV news stations.

When she was done, Fox said, "Well, let's spend the next half hour on tomorrow's speech. Figured I'd ask you to produce the first draft."

With that, he provided the high points he wanted to cover as well as describing the tone he hoped to achieve. After this commentary was done, he said, "Let's meet at noon to review the draft. I plan to keep my remarks to about 15 minutes and provide another 15 for the press in attendance."

Once they'd signed off, David said, "Let's eat. Then, you can get started. You get your choice between an omelet or a sandwich."

"The sandwich," she said and gave him a hug in thanks for his ongoing support.

The Speech

Jen had spent the better part of the night and all morning articulating Fred Fox's desire to achieve a totally separate, self-sustaining society.   Certainly, Pennsylvania's declaration of independence was the first key step, but the closing of the border, at least in his mind, was a close second.

While he understood the risks and recognized that PA could not currently stand alone and would, therefore, experience some temporary pain, he had a very apocalyptic vision of the direction the world had been heading under the United States. He also believed that some new version of the U.S. would ultimately replace the four independent countries unless each took steps to become self-reliant with no dependence upon others.

Frankly, he welcomed the isolation that others feared and had his own definition of the so-called "dark ages." To him, a lack of cultural exchange could become a positive, and he felt that the "darkness" came from people losing touch with meaningful values.

Trends like materialism and caste consciousness were at the heart of darkness – not a society getting back in touch with all that mattered.

So, that had been Jen's assignment for the night – trying to communicate all of that in 15 minutes plus details about the closing of the border.

"Good effort," Fox finished reading the draft.

"You sure we haven't gone too far in explaining to people where you want PA to land?" Jen asked. "Philosophical arguments tend to lose people, and don't forget you have some pretty militant factions both in Pennsylvania and neighboring countries."

"By closing the border." Fox stated, "we've taken an important freedom from people and made their lives much less convenient and complete. I think folks deserve an explanation with regard to why."

"An abstract goal – whether right or wrong – won't be good enough to satisfy these people," Jen argued. "You will have given them ammunition for expressing their discontent without accomplishing what you hoped."

"Jen, you sound so cynical! What have we done to you?" Fox laughed and joked while still sending a serious message and not taking back his words.

When Jen and David met for lunch, she recapped the session to review the speech. Though invited, David had been unable to attend due to a conflict with another meeting.

Sitting in a booth at a small, nearby diner, Jen summarized her concerns, ending, "I don't think he has any idea how many enemies he's accumulated over the past few years."

"I know he doesn't care about that, Jen."

"The situation is becoming dangerous."

"More dangerous than those we've already been through?"

"Not *more* maybe," Jen said, "but different."

Eating in companionable silence with their own thoughts, David finally said, "Tell you what. I'll mention those concerns to the chief risk officer. He's in charge of security and can decide whether he needs to step up our precautions."

"Be sure to explain that these remarks will be different from past ones – more likely to incite," which was her way of agreeing with David's strategy.

"Am I overreacting?" she asked. "You've read the speech."

"Maybe a bit," David said, "but I could be underreacting. I'm told I'm prone to doing that. Still, we'll give the Risk group the warning, and we'll have put matters into the right hands." Pausing, he then added, "The speech is good and does try to explain that the sacrifice of a certain freedom of movement is not for nothing. Unfortunately, I think Fox will find most people are motivated by protecting the conveniences of their daily lives."

"Think he's right?" Jen asked.

"That's another matter," David laughed. "I'm very much on board with keeping Pennsylvania independent. Therefore, I do believe that self-sufficiency is essential. However, I think that has to evolve organically as folks live their new lives and recognize qualities worth maintaining. While closing our border will create new needs, I don't see that action providing solutions. That said, Fred Fox is a very smart man – much smarter than I am. So, I'm willing to defer to his judgement. Besides, we probably won't know the outcome for quite a long time."

With that, Jen and David walked back to their apartment. "I'm taking the dog out," David said, "and then have a meeting with Fox – probably something to do with his speech."

"If he says we should attend in person?" Jen asked.

"We get back on a helicopter."

Turned out, Jen and David did not have to fly back to Harrisburg – largely because Fox kept revising his message right up to the last minute and needed them immediately available, which could be better accomplished from home than from a moving helicopter.

As a result, Jen and David joined a large portion of Penndelom in watching the speech on the local arena's 20-foot jumbotron.

As he spoke, you could see people turning to those sitting next to them, making comments, and asking questions. The audience – initially still – grew restless, and a low murmur seemed to pass among the crowd in a wave.

Hostility?

No.

Confusion?

Yes.

Unsure whether they'd heard Fox's message correctly, David assumed the source of their confusion was disbelief.

However, they didn't seem angry – at least not yet.

They weren't especially militant.

They just seemed puzzled.

"Hey, Dave," a nearby voice called out, "he doesn't really mean I can't go visit my daughter in Northeasterly, does he?"

"Yes. That's exactly what he means. At least you can't visit her without special permission and an official pass."

"No."

"Yes."

"Can't be."

"You need to understand, Fox is trying to look at the long-term good. Protecting our children's future."

"Meaning maybe I'll get to visit my unborn grandchild on her 10th birthday?"

"Come on folks. Give him a chance," David said to those nearby. "Fox has not steered us wrong yet and deserves to get the benefit of the doubt. Probably won't be as bad in reality as many of you are already imagining."

"Too much too soon?" Jen asked David as they slowly walked home and gradually separated from the crowd.

"People get entrenched in their habits. Fox recognizes that and was trying to make his move before that happened. I actually expected worse."

"Fox will be calling in an hour for our debrief," Jen reminded him. "I'm sure he'll ask for our assessment of the crowd in Penndelom."

"More bewildered than hostile, though that could change soon."

"Well, we already know the reactions of other countries, so I guess we wait and see."

"Could have been worse," Fox summarized, "and probably unlikely to have been better than what we got."

"Proper enforcement of the action will be critical," David noted.

"David, I heard your old friend John has turned up in Southwesterly. Think he plans to stay? Think he'd be interested in a new job? He'd be able to handle his duties from home."

"Full time?" David wondered

"Wouldn't necessarily have to be," Fox replied. "I'm more interested in getting some work accomplished than in making sure 40 hours per week are spent."

"I know he likes his current teaching job," David warned.

"I think he could probably do both. Can you set up a video conference?

John's New Job

With the closing of PA's borders and Northeasterly already choosing to do likewise, Fred Fox was anticipating a need to put some new informal channels of communication into place. While none of the four infant countries had yet to establish a diplomatic corps, the kind of role Fred Fox anticipated requiring was that sort of person-to-person contact that would have been orchestrated by an ambassador, often using a junior staff member as the actual courier.

While Fox did not believe a whole department needed to be established and wasn't sure a senior-level person was necessary, he kind of liked the idea of having that lower-level staff member available to handle certain errands.

Although Fox had no immediate assignment for a person in Southwesterly, he knew the right candidate did not come around every day, so he put the wheels in motion to recruit John O'Hara. Born in PA, a decorated member of the military during the recent war for independence, and now seemingly on his way to building a new life in Southwesterly, John was a perfect fit for Fox's new role. Frankly, he would never consider an "outsider" who had fewer ties to PA in such a sensitive capacity, and even then, he would never test that person with any request that involved picking one allegiance over the other. While some risk was involved, the potential benefit could someday be great.

Since he wasn't in any way asking John to compromise his new loyalty to Southwesterly, and was ideally after an individual who was, in fact, loyal to both countries, Fox believed he might interest O'Hara, who still had some friends and family in PA.

A peacemaker, not a spy. That was Fox's vision.

While he knew David Evans and John O'Hara had a long history and understood that particular connection was part of his interest in John – like an unsolicited personal reference – Fox would not ask David to make the offer to his friend.

"Why me?" John asked.

"My instinct tells me you can be trusted."

"So, you want me to be a spy?"

"No," Fox corrected him, "just a messenger. Should the need arise, I might want someone in place who could personally deliver a sensitive, verbal message to the powers that be. More than likely, the contact would be such that I wouldn't want a printed or electronic copy hanging around waiting to be found. Furthermore, I expect such a message would be in the best interests of both Pennsylvania and Southwesterly." His basic request made, Fox shifted gears a bit, "I understand that you are rebuilding a new life, and I'm not looking to interfere with that. By the way, congratulations. I'm told you have a new child on the way." Sensing that John still needed more convincing, Fox explained, "To make such a role work, I believe you would have to be formally introduced to certain people from Southwesterly as a trusted source who can be counted upon to speak my thoughts as though they came directly from my mouth."

"Man. I don't know," John seemed both troubled and somewhat agitated. "I never heard of such a job."

"Maybe the word 'job' is throwing you," Fox interjected. "Let's use the word 'role'. Many new needs are arising that didn't exist before."

"Can I take some time to think about this request?" John hedged.

"Absolutely."

"Okay to get my friend David's thoughts?"

"Him, yes," Fox answered. "However, no one else. If too many people know, your effectiveness could be compromised."

"Joanna?"

"I wouldn't, but that's your decision. I realize you'll do what you feel is best regardless of my answer."

"Understood," John said and realized that if he told Joanna, he shouldn't tell Fox.

"By the way, you would receive a small monthly honorarium."

"David, did Fox explain this goofy new role he wants to put into place . . . with me as the initial goof?" John asked.

"Yes. He does like to look ahead and plan for a rainy day."

"Assuming he is serious and has really described the new role accurately, why should I?"

"I don't think you should feel in any way obligated. You've paid your dues and almost gave PA a leg in the process already. Furthermore, your future is elsewhere. So, you have no real reason to do as he asks. The money, while something, is not enough to be much of a factor, though I suspect money would never be an important part of the equation for you."

"Gotta tell you, David, you're quite the salesman," John offered sarcastically.

"Both you and Joanna have good jobs with stable, promising futures. You'd be foolish to jeopardize that."

"You are clearly trying your damnedest to talk me into this challenge," John's sarcasm continued. "If I'm really just a messenger boy to be used on a limited number of occasions with very specific circumstances, why not?"

"I do believe Fox is trustworthy," David noted, "and that you can take his word to the bank."

"I just kind of wish he'd never asked."

"I get that. Take your time to consider the matter. Who knows, maybe the whole issue will just fade away, though I don't really think that will be the case."

John did have some divided loyalties. Although his future was out west and he was very comfortable with this new world he now embraced as his own, he felt a "No" answer to Fox would be a repudiation of his past – his history, his family, his sacrifices, and his friends. As a result, he needed to take the path that best allowed him to celebrate both his past and future.

"Okay," John said to Fred Fox. "I'll do as you ask but with the understanding that I can pull out at any time."

"That's fine," Fox felt comfortable agreeing largely because of John's military record – O'Hara was not a person to back out unless he had a very good reason.

"So, what's the next step?" John wondered.

"I will ask you to have a brief meeting with two Southwesterly heads of state to make sure they will recognize you should the time and need ever materialize. I will see that each of them gets a personal introduction of sorts from me without me having to travel or communicate with them through formal channels. Then, you are basically done unless and until a circumstance arises."

"This better be on the up and up."

"You can count on that," Fox stated.

"I am," John responded.

Looking Backward

Life in the post-revolutionary world was – of necessity – lived on a smaller scale than within the old United States. History now suggests that this trend was a necessary correction that was generally accepted, embraced, and endured – depending upon the individual – as both good and as a handicap in many ways. At least in the infancy of this new existence, many people enjoyed the novelty of a different, slightly slower, perhaps less complicated way of life, though signs of discontent – felt as a nagging sense of missing out on some unknown opportunity that everyone else was able to enjoy – never completely went away for a segment of the population. The mantra "bigger is better" was still too fully ingrained within that group, though few of them would be able to articulate what exactly was now missing from their daily existence.

Living Life on a Smaller Scale

With the ultimate closing of borders among the newly formed nations, travel was limited so people contented themselves with lives confined to lesser spaces. While this change created an increasingly parochial attitude and outlook for some, movement within that reduced area was no longer monitored by a massive central government computer system. So, a greater sense of freedom was gained. In the eyes of many, this tradeoff was worthwhile.

The 9 to 5 Work-a-day World

With large companies forced to reduce their operations due to new political constraints that increased the costs of doing business, jobs became less impersonal and individuals a bit more indispensable within a shrinking labor pool.

When a senior worker with 10 years of experience expressed discontent about a dress-code requirement or another highly skilled technician suggested a new vending machine for the employee lunchroom, management was quick to comply – especially to requests that could be easily and relatively inexpensively granted. New formal paths to promotion were carved out; rewards were earned for new employee referrals; work schedules were reduced with many people electing four 10-hour days to have a long weekend. The balance of power had clearly shifted somewhat in the direction of the worker.

Climate Change and the New Neighborhood-Based Social Structure

Though still too new to measure accurately, significant improvement to the ongoing climate change crisis was a side benefit of the world's gradual transformation. Small plots of green space were turning up as more and more people turned to gardening for both food and recreation. While these plots were quite tiny, they nevertheless were starting to soften a harsh landscape of glass and concrete.

Sometimes, neighbors would combine their garden areas with those of their friends next door. Therefore, daily maintenance became a shared activity and recreational opportunity. The harvest was split 50/50 and celebrated with a joint feast. When bad weather threatened a community crop, everyone met to share ideas for meeting the crisis. A neighborhood-based social structure was re-emerging. While more time and even more gardens would be needed to reverse adverse climate change, air-quality studies suggested that the past century-long failure as nature's caretakers might be slowly turning around. As a bonus, reduced travel lessened fossil fuel emission.

Education

Since closed borders were making any kind of multi-country life exceedingly difficult, students were forced to attend colleges within their own nations – even though that limited areas of study and eventual vocational opportunities at companies dealing with shrinking labor pools. While the old technology still existed, equipment repairs were often not possible, and new breakthroughs in science were scarce.

Although every new country had quite a few colleges and could continue to graduate doctors, nurses, engineers, teachers, etc. – a young man from Hazelton, PA, who planned to become a physician, found that he was 110th in line for placement into 100 openings. As a result, he became a veterinarian because he did manage to make that cut, but such a flexible change of career path did not help offset the shortage of doctors expected to occur in just a few years.

At the lower K – 12 levels, large consolidations began to breakup into their original community school districts, which were more practical to sustain within this new world. While the schools lacked the staff or financial resources to support the electives previously available . . . a strong town spirit was cultivated, which strengthened the relationship among those located in close physical proximity.

Front Porches as the New Social Media

As in the past – especially in larger cities – neighborhoods played a much more significant part in people's lives and were, in fact, once again the center of society. Social media, which still existed, was no longer a particularly common or important way of interacting with each other on a daily basis and was relegated to providing a means of interacting with the people of the various new countries, though the large, centralized servers needed to support even that reduced level of activity had started to fail.

In the time before the great secession and subsequent reorganization, few people knew their neighbors. Most hurried head down from one location to the next, carefully checking and rechecking the security card that would allow entrance into the next building. These days, after-work strolls for pleasure had become very common. Men and women of all ages enjoyed walking and hearing the calls of greeting across the street to both pedestrians and others sitting on their porches.

Life on a smaller scale was both a look back and forward.

195

Fred Fox

Fred Fox was not a lifetime politician. In fact, he had an entire successful career as a research scientist before running for his first public office. Even then, he started by winning the race for Pennsylvania governor without having to rise through the local ranks.

So why – when most of his contemporaries were retiring – was Fred interested in starting a second career?

The answer to that question was not so simple. Part of the reason was just because he could. He was wealthy enough to afford the luxury of politics without having to build a network of financial and political support in advance. Another part of the answer was that he'd grown tired of the stupidity and incompetence he was seeing throughout the country but particularly in the state capitol of Harrisburg. The final piece of the puzzle was probably not the most significant but the one most frequently cited – altruism. He wanted to contribute. He wanted to help.

Fred grew up in a modest middle-class family – firm believers in the continued existence of the American Dream. He was taught that he could accomplish anything. He was taught that hard work and effort were rewarded. For the most part, that belief had proven true for him.

He worked hard in school – academically and in sports – and had been given a scholarship to a good university he could not otherwise have afforded. Again, he worked hard in college and excelled – graduating from Brown and then Rensselaer with Latin after his name, Magna not Summa. During an on-campus visit by potential employers, he had an interview with a recruiter for a large pharmaceutical company that offered him – prior to his graduation – a high-paying job doing research.

Fox yet again excelled and was part of a team instrumental in developing a critical, *and* lucrative, new drug for his employer. He eventually became a team leader and made quite a lot of money that was invested wisely, including one stock in particular that grew by several hundred percent and helped make him a millionaire by the age of 50.

Eventually, Fox realized the time had come to retire. Technology and science in his field had begun to outstrip his education, and he did not have sufficient enthusiasm to go back to school. He had never been one to ride the coattails of others to achieve success.

Fox very well might have become a complacent retiree – had a different president other than King been in office.

Frankly, the man's attitude and idiocy confounded and infuriated him. While Fox was not in a position to run for a national political office, he set his sights on the top job in PA.

Fred Fox was not a fan of the current version of society in the United States. He found the heavily centralized government to be overbearing and felt the extreme measures that had been put into place in the name of security were excessive and spirit-deadening. Every overture to institute change within the system was immediately stifled. After this cycle was repeated a half dozen times, Fox began exploring other avenues for change.

Needless to say, Penndelom's declaration of independence from the U.S. and Pennsylvania caught him off guard, or he would have attempted some pre-emptive negotiations. Philosophically, he was on the same page as the so-called revolutionaries, and both certainly shared a dislike for the policies and values of President King.

Fox knew he was in a minority in welcoming isolationism. While he kept hearing that such a posture would lead to a new age of regression and decline, he frankly welcomed that as a possible return to a less sophisticated value structure that featured a simpler, more indigenous way of life. He believed the world needed to take several steps back in order to move forward.

While discussions and behind-the-scenes activities prompting PA's declaration of independence had been underway for some time, Penndelom's announcement had come at a very unfortunate juncture. Fox did not feel adequately prepared to act, but he felt very strongly that all of PA had to present a unified front and that Penndelom could not be allowed to go their separate way.

So, Fred Fox took a deep breath and gambled that he could still get away with PA's premature announcement. However, he knew he needed some luck. For instance, he was counting on King's ego being so large that he could not even conceive of the possibility that a state would secede under his watch, even though only a deaf man could have missed the many rumblings coming from all sides of the country.

Fox knew other states were in discussions similar to those of PA. However, he was still very surprised when Southwesterly unveiled a cohesive separation by eight states that were choosing to form their own regional country. While Fox envied the strength of such a unified front, he did not regret PA's decision to go forward alone. In the end, he felt his corner of the world would end up being a better place.

By moving PA's declaration up, he was able to leverage Penndelom's decision to remain part of the state. During that time, he got to know the community's principal players who were previously unknown to him.

Specifically, Ron Rose and David Evans appeared to be the key individuals.

Watching the broadcasts of events back in Penndelom and his own family's reactions, Fox concluded that Rose – the actual head of the successful movement – was a traditional labor leader and politician. He was well known by the people and very popular. And yet, the young man who presented the new Penndelom flag somehow stole the show. He had a charismatic quality that seemed to attract people to him, seeking his approval.

Fox found this person interesting and the key to bringing Penndelom back into the fold.

Unfortunately, he wasn't quite sure about the best way to sway Evans over to his side.

He tried to buy him with the promise of a highly placed position, but Evans refused and pointed Fox in Rose's direction.

He then tried including Evans' girlfriend in the offer, which seemed to help but was not enough without further enticement. Interestingly, she turned out to be a real bargain and one of his best decisions to date. However, Fox's big breakthrough came from an unexpected source.

Quite fortuitously, President King took matters out of his hands by making multiple bad decisions that forced David into full cooperation with Fox.

Thus far, Fred found David to be loyal and conscientious. Personal gain played no part in his decisions and actions. He really was just a humble guy trying to do the right thing – allowing his own thoughts to determine what was right.

When Ron Rose was killed, David became second in command in PA, which Fox knew the young man found to be troubling. He believed himself to be too young and inexperienced for that role, and most of Fox's enemies would agree.

While Fox was fully expecting David to resign from that job and was trying to find the right leverage to keep him on the team, Fox was impressed by the effective way he carried out several difficult assignments.

On the night Fox made his speech about the closing of the PA borders, he could tell Evans was troubled.

"What's the problem, David?"

"I'm not sure I have one. However, I know you've got a great vision for a new world and understand that the decision about the borders is part of that, but I'm not so sure I see the same outcome as you," he responded. "Some powerful forces are being unleashed by our actions. Just look at how quickly Northeasterly responded. And Fred, watch your back. Some of those dissident radicals want your head."

"They've wanted that for some time."

"But now," David warned, "they've got a cause with some emotional energy attached. With families being separated, the radicals are gaining mainstream support. I repeat. Watch your back. Add some extra security. I don't want your wife to become a widow."

"Not like you to be so melodramatic," Fox commented.

"I'm trying to find the words to make you hear me."

Although the world was just now in the process of reacting to Fox's speech the previous evening, the action by PA appeared to have a surprisingly unsettling effect that rippled across North America. Specifically, Fox had suddenly stripped people of the illusion of the basics of daily life being largely unchanged despite the fact that history was rewritten.

Being a good man, Fox found the reaction of his citizens to be unsettling, even troubling. Still, he was convinced his vision of the future was the right one and that the actions taken were necessary to realize that dream.

A few days after Fox's border-closing speech, he had been prescheduled to make a number of personal appearances – a mall opening, a major sporting event, and a fund-raising telecast.

Such duties seldom bothered Fred, who often found them energizing. He was one of those people who was good at using the energy of others to jump-start his own battery. In this particular instance, he was especially looking forward to the opportunity to gauge the reactions of people outside his administration to his announcement.

The first stop at the mall was uneventful. In fact, Fox realized current malls had changed so dramatically, a new word was probably be needed to better describe them and set appropriate expectations. Rather than a large, enclosed structure housing countless self-contained retail stores, this new mall was far more like an open-air market – a combination of small specialty shops and a large number of food and produce vendors as well as entertainment. While Fox knew such places had always existed and were destination shopping areas for some people, every town now seemed to sport some smaller scaled-down version of these "Malls."

Today's Grand Opening was special because the new facility was on the outskirts of Penndelom, and Fox still felt a need to cultivate that audience and prove himself to them. David and Jen, back in Penndelom, were to meet Fox and his wife, Elizabeth, to provide a bit of a tour prior to the ribbon-cutting ceremony.

"Good trip?" David called Fox as they all moved toward the stage at the front of the large facility.

"Just fine. We've got helicopter rides to each of today's events. What do I need to know about this one?"

"Nothing. Very harmless," David responded. "The mall is a very welcome addition that reduces local dependency upon goods from other places. You are getting lots of credit for providing much of the funding. You may see a few protestors – mostly people who now have relations in different countries they can no longer easily visit – but I don't expect local reaction to be too intense."

David was correct in his assessment. The brief ceremony went off without incident.   Jen introduced Fox and his wife while David disappeared into the background. Fox said his few words, and they all went off for lunch at the facility with local dignitaries. By 1:00, the four of them were boarding the helicopter to go to a baseball game in the western part of PA.

The sporting event attended by Fox and his group was a minor league baseball game in Erie. A few years back, the city was awarded a franchise affiliated with the Pittsburgh Pirates, and the town was still filled with rabid supporters in the early throngs of the honeymoon period – team loyalty perhaps heightened by the fact that 90% of the games now involved international play among the four countries that used to be part of the United States.

David and Jen felt wary of the crowd and the minimal amount of security, but the group ventured forth.

A warm, sunny summer day with a cool breeze, it was perfect baseball weather. Sitting on the so-called party deck, which was somewhat like the minor league version of a luxury box, the four of them each had their obligatory ballpark hot dog shortly before the 7th inning stretch.

When the loudspeaker announced the special guest in attendance, the news was met with a combination of cheers and jeers. Fred Fox was rapidly becoming a polarizing force. However, he drew a round of applause when he donned an Erie baseball hat and saluted the Erie pitcher.

Fred Fox always knew how to work a crowd.

At the end of the 7th, the group had to move on to catch their flight to the final appointment of the day – the fundraising telecast originating from Allentown.

The flight did not take long, but the afternoon had become evening during the process of getting to the airport and waiting for hours for permission to lift off. As a result, the last leg of the journey was done in total darkness, which always seemed somehow different in a helicopter – more isolating and eerie – more aware of being in a fairly small and fragile refuge against the night.

Once cleared for landing, the helicopter set down, and a long, dark limousine waited to take them to the television station for the telethon.

The trip started uneventfully, but – about 20 minutes later – the driver steered them onto a suspiciously deserted road.

"Driver, are you sure you didn't take a wrong turn?" Jen asked.

Silence.

As all the passengers began to share her concern – which slowly elevated to alarm – Fox attempted to use his cell phone to make a call to the three security vehicles accompanying them – but got no signal.

"What happened to the secret service assigned to the trip?" Fox's wife asked.

"They were in the cars immediately behind us and had probably checked out the driver before we even got into the limo, but we must have lost all three vehicles at about the time we turned off onto this road.

Our tracking-device signal was cellular and seems to have gone the same way as our phones – silent."

As the car pulled over, the panel separating front from back opened slightly, and the driver said, "Everyone but Fox needs to get out. He's the only one we need, and we're not out to harm anyone unnecessarily."

"Do as he said," Fox instructed.

"I'll stay with you and the car," David insisted and then pounded on the glass panel to announce his intention.

"No. You need to get out now. If you don't, everyone will get hurt," the driver responded.

"Go, David," Fox commanded. "I don't want to risk my wife and Jen becoming collateral damage."

"I hear you, Fred, but don't be a hero when I get out. We need you."

Standing in the middle of the deserted road, David, Jen, and Elizabeth Fox hesitated before slowly starting to retrace their steps back in the direction of the main road.

"We all warned Fred about security," Fox's wife stated. "He was convinced such measures were unnecessary in this brave new world."

After the three of them had walked along the road for about an hour, Jen announced as she successfully got a call through to the security team in Harrisburg, "Finally! Cell phone service."

"Thank God," the duty officer responded. This place has been crazy since the security detail reported you missing."

"Fred is not with us," Jen stated. "We got hijacked and left at the side of the road; he was taken away – we don't know where."

"Is he okay?"

"So far as we know."

"And the rest of you are unharmed?"

"Yes. We're fine."

"We've tried to put a trace on any of your phones

but have had no success. We'll try again now that you are in cell phone range."

Waiting for contact from the abductors, Chief Risk Officer Perry Adams ordered security to get Fox's wife, Jen, and David back to Harrisburg. Unable to serve any useful purpose where they were, the group agreed to return as Adams recommended.

"We should have heard something by now. Some sort of demand," Elizabeth Fox wondered aloud. "Right?"

"Maybe not," David tried to be reassuring and as positive as possible, though he secretly agreed. Frankly, he feared the operation was carried out by a bunch of amateurs, which worried him. Too many ways for plans to go wrong. "Fred is resourceful. Maybe he's made some sort of suggestion that's got them stuck in an internal debate."

Jen then said, "The press has gotten wind. I guess as soon as the telethon appearance got cancelled, some reporters got suspicious – or maybe even were tipped off— and began reaching out to their contacts. I need to make a statement. Any suggestions?"

"A low-key version of the truth," David said. "We have no choice."

With that, Jen went off to deal with the waiting journalists, and Fox's wife returned to their residence.

David took a slow walk over to Adams' office, "No word yet?"

"No," the chief risk officer stated.

"Isn't that strange?"

"I think so," said the CRO. "Not a good sign."

"Any leads on the perpetrators?" David asked. "I know a radical element in Northeasterly has wanted Fox's head."

"Yes. That group is our primary suspect."

Both men mulled the situation in silence when Adams said, "You know, David, over six hours have already passed. Though we have very few specific rules spelled out yet for a succession plan, you probably need to be sworn in as an interim; you are the second in command."

Silence.

David?"

Silence.

"Not yet. We don't have any specific need to exercise authority right now, so no immediate action needs to be taken. Let's wait."

"Interim," the CRO repeated for emphasis.

"Let's wait."

"Okay, Dave, but you probably only have until noon, and judicial might even think that was way too long. We can't ignore the necessity."

"How did the press conference go, Jen?"

"Awful. They're looking for answers – understandably – and we have none. They also started talking about contingency plans – as in succession – and we have none. Have you given any thought to the matter?"

"Our chief risk officer has informed me that I have until noon to put off answering that question."

At 11:00 AM, Harrisburg officially received word from the captors that Fred Fox had been assassinated. As they were given instructions about where the body could be reclaimed, they were told that officials from Northeasterly would be contacting the designated interim government of PA with a new offer of consolidation. Clearly, they had found Fox a difficult negotiator.

The CRO immediately sent a security detail to reclaim the body and investigate the circumstances, asking them to do their best in coming up with a reconstruction of events.

Adams then let Fox's widow know what had taken place and promised further details once the team arrived back.

A strong woman, who'd already overcome many challenges in life, Fred's wife had apparently sensed a need to prepare herself for the worst and took the news in stride. Already addressing the many practical needs of the moment, she became a first lady in first lady mode, recognizing that many arrangements had to be made.

The CRO and David then spoke with Jen to craft a press statement, but not before David was informed, "You have no choice, Dave. You've got to be sworn into office now, or PA has no official government."

"Perry," he appealed to the CRO, "you know as well as I do, that I'm no Fred Fox and not equipped to deal with the demands of this job for even a short period of time. I'm too young. I'm too inexperienced. I told the same to Fred many times. In fact, I've just been waiting for the right time to find the best way and opportunity to resign."

"Well, he apparently did not agree, and Fred was a very good judge of character. You do see that we have no choice, right? If you'd feel better, we can call you an interim and then consult the various factions to iron out the terms of a more formal succession plan."

"Perry, I'm really not trying to be difficult."

"Just a natural, huh," Adams said.

"David," Jen stated, "Perry is right. We are currently on a ship adrift with no one steering. Let him swear you in as the interim CEO."

Silence.

David – not in any way comfortable with these developments and simultaneously grieving over the loss of a friend – recognized the inevitability of these actions and suddenly saw his future spiraling out of his control. However, he knew he had no choice and also recognized that all progress of the last two and a half years could be lost immediately, and he didn't want the sacrifices of Fred and others to be in vain.

"Let's put a six-month maximum time limitation on the interim. At that time, an election must take place to name the new CEO."

"We can try," the CRO stated, "but a new election was never discussed or mandated."

"I bet most people from all sides will embrace that course of action as being the least objectionable of the alternatives."

"You'll be stuck negotiating with Northeasterly as a lame duck."

"An election should in no way limit our choices with them," David responded.

"Sooooo," Jen said. "I guess I better meet with the press."

"Only *after* he is sworn into office. We've got to keep confusion to the minimum."

The next few days passed in a whirlwind.

The security detail returned with Fox's body. While they explained that any theory about reconstruction of events was pure guesswork, they speculated that Fox had tried to escape and was accidentally killed by startled guards during the process.

Fox's widow constructed an official, highly dignified state funeral with representatives from Southwesterly, Midwesterly, and even Northeasterly attending.

In her eulogy and various other statements to the press, she emphasized that her husband had been the number one supporter of David Evans and felt confident that the country was being left in capable hands ready and able to carry out their shared vision of the future.

David, in turn, met with various government officials and developed an official succession plan that made the Deputy CEO the interim CEO only until an official, country-wide election could be held in six months.

David met with his contacts from various countries and called upon his old friend John O'Hara – in his new capacity – to deliver a quiet message to Southwesterly. Specifically, he explained that PA was under pressure from Northeasterly to join their union, which they did not want to do. As a result, David was asking whether he could count upon their support – military and otherwise – should the issue come to a confrontation requiring action.

Needless to say, David was grateful to Fred Fox for his foresight in putting this important line of communication into place.

Despite pressures to do so, David and Jen would not relocate to Harrisburg. They continued to maintain a primary residence in Penndelom and commute back and forth to the capitol, staying over several nights a week.

"Six months," David said. "We can do this for six months. You can do anything for six months. Right, Jen?"

"Of course," she agreed. "Though who knows what will happen then."

"Meanwhile," David said, "I don't think people fully understand how critical Fred Fox was to PA's future. In the end, his vision may have been shortened with his assassination. The force of his personality was the glue that held this nation together."

"Then," Jen said, "your job for the next six months will be to pick up the pieces and put them back together. Maybe not in exactly the same way as Fred's plan but in a good way nonetheless. He'd understand the need to adapt to reality."

Daily Herald OpED

Signing Off
by Dr. Garfield Payne – Professor
Political Science
Penndelom Community College

For those of you who read my previous article, you will not be surprised to learn that this editorial will be my last for the Daily Herald. Faced with the choice of either being unable to visit our son or relocating to his country of Midwesterly, my wife and I have chosen the latter. However, we do so with many regrets because we have very much enjoyed our life within Penndelom and Pennsylvania, and I am grateful to the newspaper for providing me with this platform for my views. That said, this parting editorial is my tribute to Fred Fox.

Grief . . . and Then Depression

Just when the world was starting to show some signs of stability, that very tentative balance of past, present, and future was shattered – at least in Pennsylvania – by the assassination of CEO Fred Fox. The fact that he had a clear vision of the way he wanted the Independent Nation of Pennsylvania to evolve had helped steer people in the right direction without them being overtly aware of his guiding hand.

David Evans has always been among those who recognized this remarkable talent of Fred's, and he has been acutely aware that very few people could do likewise. I know for a fact that he does not feel equipped to fill the role of carrying out Fred's vision even on a temporary basis. However, I personally believe he is wrong and does not give himself enough credit. We are fortunate that he will be the one guiding PA into the future.   That said, the loss of Fred is felt on a daily basis and can be witnessed in innumerable ways.

Most people now have less faith in our ability to remain independent. Fred had inspired that confidence. Similarly, coffee shop conversation now assumes PA will join Northeasterly – with the main question being when. School-age students find themselves less focused on preparing for a future that suddenly seems very uncertain, and parents can no longer convince themselves to apply pressure on their children because they, too, see the time ahead as dark and murky. While people still go to work each day, they arrive barely on time and leave promptly at 5:00 — or even a few minutes before when circumstances allow – feeling any extra above-and-beyond effort is wasted. Finally, people have stopped watching the news because they expect more disappointment and instead go listlessly through the motions of life.

In other words, the new Independent Nation of Pennsylvania appears to me to be experiencing a great depression – both economic and psychological. My parting gift to you my friends is this observation in the hope that you will do Fred the honor of living by his example – a life of optimism and faith in the future. He would want that and would also urge you to give David Evans a chance.

Picking Up the Pieces

The day was once again gray. There had been no sunshine for weeks, and dark rain clouds hovered perpetually overhead. Plus, the sight of "heat lightening" in the distance hinted at the relief of rain, but the temperatures remained stifling hot.

No landscape could look more grim, dirty, and depressed against such a backdrop, and neither Penndelom nor Harrisburg were exceptions.

Since the death of Fred Fox, nine out of ten days seemed to have this gloomy pall – as though the Earth had also gone into a state of mourning. The new official PA flag flew at half-mast everywhere, and an amazing number of citizens of PA had taken the additional step of creating their own memorials ranging from hanging his picture within a black border to placing black crosses in their front windows and leaving bouquets of flowers in their yards.

Fred had successfully communicated a sense of optimism about the future as well as confidence and faith in people's ability to realize their dreams. He got them to believe that small *could* be beautiful and had made just enough progress toward the achievement of his goals that people could point to these early successes as proof.

The feeling in the national capitol of Harrisburg was the worst. Walking the corridors of their offices from one department to the next, you had the sense that all the computers were involved in job searches with most of the targeted locations being in neighboring countries.

Frankly, David Evans agreed.

The early polls clearly showed that David was by far the people's choice to succeed Fred Fox. However, those same polls showed that they had far less faith in David's ability to carry out Fox's plans than they had in Fred's ability to succeed. The majority clearly believed only Fred could complete his vision for PA's future and that people were only on board with that course of action while Fred was the captain steering the boat.

Again, David basically agreed.

The country had voted overwhelmingly to adopt David's suggestion of an interim CEO for six months prior to a new election to select Fred's replacement. The question in David's mind was how he should behave during his tenure as the "interim." Should he be a mere caretaker of the status quo, even though the status quo was far too new to carry much weight as a precedent? Or, should he try to advance Fred's vision to the next logical step – further severing trade ties with neighboring countries? Perhaps David should rethink the whole equation and try to figure out for himself an appropriate next course of action. Then again, maybe his imagination just was not good enough to even see the next critical step that needed to be taken.

Meanwhile, Northeasterly had completely severed trade channels with PA, and the radical element of that country – one of whom assassinated Fred Fox – seemed to be gaining strength with the annexation of PA as the principal issue propelling their popularity. On top of everything else, the craziest among the extremists kept implying that – unless David cooperated – he would be next.

Fortunately, Southwesterly continued to be an important ally. Their military support of PA might, in fact, have been the only deterrent to an invasion by Northeasterly.

While Southwesterly was diplomatically critical, David – regrettably – could not picture any further synergy between the two countries. While PA's borders were closed to Southwesterly, very little trade had occurred between them, so the loss was not great.

However, this circumstance was not the case with Midwesterly.

PA was very dependent upon them for essential food and merchandise and was, in fact, one of Fred Fox's primary targets in closing borders. He knew PA had to become less reliant upon that part of the country or had to become reconciled to being totally dependent with no leverage in wading through other political waters. Given Midwesterly's increasingly conservative makeup, this little bit of leverage mattered greatly.

"Did Fred actually have a plan for the way in which this increased self-reliance might happen?" Jen asked.

"Only sort of," David responded. "He laid the groundwork for various incentives to support agricultural and manufacturing startups, but I believe he just had faith that these, plus need, would be enough of a catalyst to stimulate the necessary solutions. For now, at least, that's the path we are continuing to pursue. The CFO says the incentives will be available next week, and we've already seen some proposals requesting funding. If half of them succeed, that would be enough to prove Fred right once again."

"David, that sounds good, but I've started to hear reports of certain food shortages. The plan you described will take time."

"I think Fred was taking a 'No pain; no gain!' posture. That was one of the parts of his plan I found lacking. He knew I disagreed."

"So, what are you going to do?" Jen asked.

"Thanks for reminding me that I need a plan and have none. I feel as though I've got all of these puzzle pieces spread out across my desk but no picture to tell me the way they fit together."

"Sorry," Jen said apologetically but stopped at the sound of a helicopter approaching.

"Guess our ride to Harrisburg just arrived," David noted.

As the chopper gained altitude, Penndelom grew smaller and smaller in the distance.

David had always lived a large part of his life within his own head, so the size of the world around him probably mattered less to him than to other people. As a result, Penndelom suited his needs just fine; being part of a world as large as Pennsylvania just added unwanted and unneeded complexity. Over the past several years, David found himself wondering what his vision of the ideal world would be. After dismissing the impulse to say, "Just like Penndelom," he'd never been able to satisfactorily answer that question.

Since he liked and trusted Fred Fox, his short-term solution had been to cast his lot with Fred's dream instead. Unfortunately, David was now finding the execution of Fox's plan to be somewhat cumbersome and unwieldy.

Once the helicopter touched down, both David and Jen had to hurry to their respective offices.

First on his agenda was a meeting with the CFO and a lobbyist group representing certain PA financial interests that were looking to convince David's administration to negotiate terms with Northeasterly but to ultimately accept Northeasterly's best offer to join that country, regardless of what those terms happened to be. While this request did not surprise him and had been heard before, David was a bit shocked to learn some new statistics about voter support for such a merger. And the source of the numbers seemed credible.

"Fred, you hear that?" David said silently to himself as the group was leaving. "What? No answer for me?"

David then prepared for his next session – a teleconference with John O'Hara.

"How goes the battle, David?" John asked to kick off the conversation.

Feeling no need to be politically correct with his old buddy from Penndelom, David confessed, "Pretty lousy. Fred Fox was a very bright man with a definite vision for this country, but he failed to leave an instruction manual for his successor."

"Doesn't sound good," John responded.

"I know I'm being unfair," David conceded. "He didn't want or plan to be assassinated. However, the fact remains, I'm basically lost."

"Well," John said, "my message for you could end up helping or hurting your chances of salvaging a good day. All depends upon your perspective."

"Oh?" he made a suspicious, non-committal sound.

"I've been asked by your old friend Marcus Marovitch to extend an offer to PA to become a permanent part of Southwesterly."

"John, between you and me, I've already considered that possibility and just can't see a way in which the alliance makes practical sense. Our countries are too different, and the geographical separation would grow troublesome very quickly. Believe me, I'd love to pass responsibility for PA's future over to Marcus and let him do the worrying, but even that gesture would be problematic."

"Marcus expected that response," John smiled sardonically, "and told me to tell you that he promised – unlike some others – not to invade PA in return."

"Sure would be nice to have that Southwesterly army standing with me at all times. I could get used to that very fast."

"You're positive then?"

"About that, yes, but be sure to tell him I was extremely grateful to get his offer."

"Ok," John agreed.

"But, John, ask Marcus whether Southwesterly might be open to a slightly less comprehensive arrangement."

"And what might that be?"

"I dunno. I haven't fully thought this through because the idea just came to me while we've been talking – but — what if PA were to become a territory of Southwesterly?"

"You mean like Puerto Rico and the Philippines were to the United States?"

"Basically. Let me take a few days to think this over and consult with some department heads. Still, gently toss the idea into the ring for Marcus to consider from his side. Then – assuming we both see some merit to the proposition – he and I could have some further discussion next week."

"Ok," John agreed, though he seemed somewhat skeptical.

"You have a problem with that?"

"Not personally. Guess I just don't see where Marcus stands to gain enough to bother. Besides," John concluded, "I suspect that won't be an easy sell to the people – either his or yours."

"The deal would structure a formal basis for defense," David said, "and would increase Southwesterly's tax base. Perhaps, and more importantly, the arrangement would keep us away from Northeasterly so they wouldn't get any stronger or perhaps more acquisitive."

"Do you want to hear about the downside now or later?" John asked.

"Later," David replied. "For now, just let me think through the possibilities."

"Sure," John responded and then joked, "Hey, man, have you ever stopped to wonder how in the hell two fairly average – though very handsome and likeable – nobodies from Penndelom ever ended up in our current positions?"

"Constantly, though it usually feels more like a nightmare than a dream."

"Hey, at least you got Jen, and I got Joanna."

"And that *does* make everything else well worth the effort."

"Hmmm. I expected our offer to be refused," Marcus Marovitch said to John, who was making his report back to Southwesterly, "but I didn't expect a quick counteroffer. A territory?" Marcus mused. "Interesting. Is Evans a strong enough leader to marshal enough support for his ideas?"

"I've learned never to underestimate the charisma of David Evans," John responded.

"A territory?" Jen restated to make sure she'd heard David correctly. "We'd be sacrificing our independence in return for some military aid and stability."

"Sounds about right. However, know that we'll lose that independence either way. If we do nothing, Northeasterly will take us by force; we just aren't strong enough to resist that. Taking this approach, we'd lose some autonomy but not all of it, and Southwesterly is much more on the same page as us. In fact, they are more of a pure democracy than PA."

"I suspect most people won't look at the matter in quite that manner," Jen commented and also added, "Fred Fox would be disappointed."

"No doubt," David agreed, "and maybe Fred could have pulled off his vision of complete independence, but I'm not Fred or enough of a politician. Think of me as a chef who is charged with the task of cooking a state dinner. I have all of these ingredients together, but I'm having trouble making a meal without his recipe. Besides, Southwesterly has less to gain than us and will probably ultimately say, 'No' after giving us a hearing."

"Relax. I'm on your side, remember?" Jen stated rhetorically. "I wouldn't want your job any more than you do, which is to say, 'Not at all.'"

"Sorry."

"I know," she said and gave him a hug, burying her face in his shoulder.

"An encrypted message just came in for you David," stated the Chief Risk Officer Perry Adams. "From the Harcastles."

"Is the decoded version ready?"

"Yes. Their contacts abroad tell them that – while our old friend King is living the high life, he keeps trying to muster an alliance of nations to strike back at the new countries formed in the wake of the United States."

"Not surprising. He's a blowhard. I'm only perplexed that the Harcastles are taking him seriously enough to bother sending a message." Then again, I remember the last time they tried to warn us,

Fox was assassinated. We might be wise to give at least some credence to what they say."

The meeting with various department heads went fine, though the session produced some unexpected responses. All of these people were handpicked by Fred Fox and extremely loyal, so they were all initially of a mind to stick as close as possible to his original vision. While discussion about becoming a territory of Southwesterly did not produce heated anger and ultimately enemies, the idea was not especially well received until the chief risk officer took David's side and explained the need to have an ally to help PA stand up to Northeasterly.

At that point, they began to give David's proposal more serious consideration.

As for him, the idea of becoming a territory made practical sense and was likely necessary at this juncture, but he could not personally feel any more enthusiastic than that. The decision – like so many – became a matter of choosing the lesser of various evils.

Quite remarkably amidst that backdrop, David's popularity remained high.

Since the assassination of Fox and taking over his new role, David's work life had become much less enjoyable. Although many aspects of his routine were unchanged, new burdens were an unwanted weight. David kept his old office and refused all suggestions to move into Fred's, so that remained the same. Similarly, his regular meetings with his direct reports stayed very similar with just a few more 'Chiefs' now being added to his list. More often than not, David still met Jen for lunch outside, and the two of them kept the small efficiency apartment they used in Harrisburg. Neither one of them had any interest in taking over the mansion and encouraged Fred's widow to remain where she was as long as David did his current job.

The biggest differences were probably subtle ones. In the past, David had been responsible for making suggestions. Now, he also had to make the accompanying decisions, knowing the wrong one had the potential to cause negative – or even disastrous – effects for many, many people.

Several weeks into his tenure as the interim CEO, he felt little had been accomplished and said as much to Jen as they returned to their capital efficiency residence.

"Cut yourself some slack. You had this situation thrust upon you with absolutely no precedent to guide you. You've done much to start the healing process of the people of PA, and you've come up with a recommendation that just might give PA a chance of survival. While Fred might have balked at becoming a territory, he was also a realist who would understand your position."

"Guess I'm most shocked to see so many people showing an interest in the upcoming election. Seems like political lines are being drawn as we speak, and new parties are being formed every hour. Since we previously had none – just an old two-party carryover that has lost meaning – I'm puzzled that recent events should produce that outcome."

"So, I assume you have not aligned yourself with a new party yet – even in your own mind?" Jen stated more than asked.

"Good God. No. I haven't *and* never will. I suspect they are unhealthy."

Arriving at their door and stepping inside, Jen said, "Always feels good to return to our second home after a long, hard day in the world. David, just remember, you are doing your job. Your primary goal has to be keeping PA up and running. All else is secondary. You set high standards and expect to accomplish more, but the most important part of your job is getting done."

Northeasterly . . . and the Value of Diplomacy

Ben and June Harcastle were very early appointments to key jobs after Northeasterly was formed. The group in power was relatively moderate, which reflected Ben and June's personal beliefs.

Practically speaking, their primary role in government was to serve as liaisons with the other new countries. However, they found that their voice was clearly heard in those days, and they successfully carved out a place in policy decision-making.

One of their earliest assignments had been to meet David Evans of PA and accompany him to Maryland. Although this piece of the mission turned out to be nothing, they did have a chance to get to know David quite well.

They found him to be somewhat enigmatic but did come to like and trust him. While Fred Fox was clearly the force to be reckoned with inside PA, they had returned home and advised all parties to work at cultivating Evans. They were quite confident he'd end up playing a significant role in PA, though they had no idea what that part might be.

As time passed, Ben and June gradually felt their influence waning as a much more radical element assumed power within Northeasterly. They had been personally devastated after hearing about the assassination of Fred Fox and were increasingly unable to have any kind of impact upon the direction of government.

While Fred Fox's assassin had acted alone and taken an initiative that was not officially sanctioned, that individual did nevertheless reflect the policies of the reigning power of the day.

The Harcastles knew David Evans had landed in a precarious spot that he would absolutely hate.

Having been involved in the shifting tides and currents of politics for many years, Ben and June felt fairly confident that their day would come again.

Weeks passed. While David made some progress with PA, he spent the majority of his time feeling frustrated. As the days marched along, he realized that PA was getting divided into three political factions. Human nature being a constant within change, David knew he shouldn't be surprised to find that groups holding diametrically opposed positions would evolve. While he consciously chose not to align himself with any party, David also realized this posture ultimately limited the power and consensus he could marshal.

After spending another long day listening to two sides argue within the legislature, David was ready to go home to Penndelom and Jen. Since Fox was killed, she traveled somewhat less frequently, which was yet another factor causing David to like his role less and less. He missed her.

Boarding the helicopter, looking up to see a thousand stars shining brightly against the purplish blue of the night sky, the pilot started the rotors and was about to take off when David suddenly realized he had forgotten a key dispatch from John O'Hara that he had promised to review over the next two days.

Disembarking, the rotors slowed as David stepped off the vehicle and flagged down his driver.

He was about to shout out his explanation when he suddenly saw a spark coming from the engine of the helicopter and felt, as much as heard, the concussive explosion as the aircraft erupted into flames.

The pilot was thrown from his seat and just managed to crawl a safe distance from the aircraft when the second and third of several smaller blasts occurred.

After getting over to the pilot and dragging him even further from the wreckage, David listened as several sirens approached and could see red and blue lights flashing as the first responders arrived on the scene.

Momentarily safe, David began to realize the bomb had been intended for him.

Watching the fire burn, David knew he had better call Jen before the event hit the news but had to hold off a bit until his hearing started to return to normal and his state of mind improved. For as much as he would like to deny that this attempt on *his life* was just a routine part of being a public figure, he'd been shaken and was trying very hard not to show it. If he'd just been a bit less responsible about going back for those files, the helicopter would have been in the air during the explosion and his future – both with Jen and in general – would most likely be gone.

Having lost both his parents unexpectedly and across a very short period of time, David had an appreciation for the fragility of life and took very little for granted. He knew for a fact that Fred Fox had not been prepared to have his time cut short but was unwilling or unable to alter his approach to life and his chosen vocation.

While David did not believe he had the kind of energy that accompanies such personal conviction, he did have a strong sense of duty that probably would always stand in his way of making smart personal choices.

Feeling somewhat more philosophical after glancing at his pilot and friend, Mitch – he finally comprehended his choices would always have the potential of helping or harming others. David's proximity to the explosion had him feeling half-deaf, but he knew he could not wait any longer to call Jen.

"Are you *sure* you're okay?"

"Both Mitch and I were lucky."

"Have they caught the culprit yet?"

"No, but everyone generally assumes the same political faction that got Fred Fox is responsible."

"Can they get you better protection?"

"Not their fault," David defended them.

"Are you going to the hospital?"

"They are making me get checked out before I'm allowed to board alternative transportation. However, I'll be home tonight; I'm just not sure when."

"David, be careful," Jen pleaded. "No foolish chances in your rush to get home."

"I promise."

Sitting at their home in Boston and having a quiet drink, Ben and June Harcastle were appalled when they heard the news about the attack.

"First Fred and now an attempt on David. We can't let this go on," June's voice trailed off with this thought.

"I know," Ben agreed. "Personally, I think most of the people of Northeasterly are moderate like us."

"If so, how did these current crazies accumulate so much power?" June asked, getting up from the couch to refill her glass.

"A fine day for a coup d'état," Ben suggested.

"Guess we'll see."

Penndelom was an especially welcome sight that night.

Having gotten checked out and requisitioned a new helicopter, David and the pilot had an uneventful flight home.

Despite her protests, David refused to let Jen meet him at the airport, but she was wide awake and waiting as he arrived home at 4:00 in the morning.

"I had to see for myself. Besides, a certain pup named Fala kept me company. He's been anxious to see you, too."

"I'm fine."

"I was so scared," she said, "and you must have been, too. I can only imagine."

"Happened too fast and suddenly to be that scary."

"And Mitch *is* okay?" she was double checking to be sure.

"I assume so. He flew us home."

"No work tomorrow," she insisted.

"We'll see. Thanks for waiting up."

"As if I wouldn't," she said and then wrapped him in the safety of her arms and held him close.

Over the course of the next several days, the aftershocks of the failed assassination attempt continued to be felt. In particular, David received a curious, unexpected note from the Harcastles apologizing for the acts of their countryman and expressing their relief that David was not hurt. The message then ended somewhat cryptically – suggesting that he continue to watch the news from the north very closely.

David's intelligence sources were telling him that some sort of uprising was underway within Northeasterly and that his old friends the Harcastles appeared to be at the center of the storm.

After calling to check on him, John O'Hara told David that their sources were corroborating the information he'd been told.

David's diplomatic contacts were paying off.

When word about the attack on David got out, the people of PA were universally outraged. However, the political lines drawn by the various factions now active in the state further coalesced around the issue of isolationism. So, despite the consensus of their reaction to David, the country was bitterly divided and increasingly split.

With an election on people's minds a few months down the road, the new parties that had formed were trying to recruit David to their ranks.

News about the successful coup d'état within Northeasterly arrived first through a private channel. Specifically, Ben and June Harcastle reached out to David to let him know that a more moderate group had successfully overthrown the radical element that had recently run the country.

The takeover was peaceful and accomplished through public distain for the radical party's methods.

Congratulating them, David promised to work closely with the Harcastles in developing a peaceful solution between the two neighbors.

"David," Ben Harcastle concluded, "one modified proposal we can extend right now is to match Southwesterly's offer to make you a territory, which we gather was the kind of relationship you preferred. Just know that Northeasterly would be happy to grant you the same situation. We get that you were trying to find a way to keep your people safe and still keep Fred Fox's dream alive."

"Thank you," David said with genuine appreciation. "Just give me some time to digest everything and meet with some people. I promise to be in touch soon."

Looking Backward

The world had changed dramatically since that New Year's Eve years ago when Penndelom chose to separate from the United States and set out on a new adventure. When a strong centralized government falls, history suggests that a difficult period typically follows.

Onset of a Darkening Age?

The decision to secede had been in direct response to a number of intolerable living conditions – not the least of which was a mind-numbing bureaucracy and suffocating control imposed by a paranoid government. Penndelom's declaration of independence and subsequent alignment with Pennsylvania had freed them of many of these ills but not without some cost. Although an overly strong national government no longer monitored or ultimately controlled every move, isolationism had begun to take over.

Initially able to cross borders among the new neighboring countries and even encouraged to do so, this free passageway slammed shut with Northeasterly and PA border restrictions that were soon adopted by Southwesterly and Midwesterly as well. Whether national pride or, perhaps, paranoia was the cause, people's worlds had shrunken and their views were becoming much narrower as both individuals and countries began to chiefly look out for themselves. Such circumstances were a clear suggestion that society was slowly slipping into a new era.

Looking back at history, a splintered world was certainly a key ingredient of change as well as the casual violence that led to a degree of barbarism in the interaction among fiefdoms. With warfare increasingly common since the violence that accompanied separation from the United States and with killing – specifically assassination – becoming a common solution for resolving political differences, the world was experiencing twilight, if not total darkness.

As the age-old saying goes, might was becoming right.

Certainly, Northeasterly initially used military strength to enlarge current borders. Although their first attempt to annex PA had failed, further initiatives occurred and more seemed likely until Ben and June Harcastle started a new reform government. While Southwesterly was an ally, some of the leadership of PA questioned whether that friendship was genuine and would last or whether they, too, would ultimately turn against a former friend.

Jen and David

"David," Ben Harcastle began, "been a long time since we last met in person."

"For all of us. You and June have certainly kept yourselves busy."

"I'm afraid this call is not strictly social. An old nemesis has resurfaced, and I'm hoping to recruit your assistance."

"Old nemesis?" David asked.

"We've heard from King. Apparently, he believes Northeasterly is in a weakened state after the recent transition in government. King has threatened to invade and occupy us as his return to power. He appears to have a couple of minor allies in place, though none of them provides enough strength to make King's threat a real one. Still . . . "

"Guess I'm not surprised; despite the fact he seemed to be totally embracing his new life."

"He's concerned about history and his legacy," Harcastle speculated.

"What can I do?" David asked.

"Our countries appear to be drifting further and further apart – concerned with their own interests and little else. In other words, we are playing right into the hands of someone like King, who wants to divide and conquer. June and I would like all of us to present a more unified front – at least to others – for our own self-preservation. As a result, we propose holding a Round Table Peace Conference in a neutral location to discuss possible terms of a mutual defense treaty. However," Ben paused to look David directly in the eye, "first, we'd like to know whether we could count on you and PA to participate."

"I believe so," David responded, "though I will need to present the concept to others before giving you a final answer."

"If you succeed," Ben stated, "and PA does join us, I have a second favor to ask. We know you are close friends with John O'Hara and have a direct line of communication to Southwesterly's leadership. Can you try to get them to participate? We really do believe all parties – except King – will benefit."

"I'll have to see where our internal discussions land, but I might be willing to do as you ask."

Hanging up the phone, David glanced out his window and saw countless people going about their daily lives – not having to think about politics, alliances, and the repercussion of every action.

He felt jealous – trapped both in a life he did not ask to have and by a future with countless responsibilities that seemed to narrow his choices. The fact that he landed in a public office mystified him. He never sought that job and was perfectly content living in a relatively small world of obscurity populated by just the handful of people who formed the core of his existence – his "group."

Nevertheless, David set the wheels in motion to have PA participate in the Round Table and had a preliminary conversation with John O'Hara.

That done, David began to pack up his work for the day and get ready for the trip back to Penndelom and Jen, who had been working from home.

Despite the fact that his fellow members of the government – specifically the various "chiefs" that now reported to him – thought he was crazy for leaving town so much with the upcoming election just a month away, David ignored the comments. However much he tried, he was unable to convince them that he really did not care about the voting and didn't want the job.

Meanwhile, several strong and outspoken factions seemed to be forming, each with a following. Basically, the country seemed to be splitting into three ideological groups. One wanted PA to keep moving forward as an independent nation, while a second would be happy being part of Northeasterly, and a third just wanted to restore some version of the old United States – remerging the four new countries into a single whole.

Looking down from his night view in the helicopter, David knew he was right not to join any of the factions even though his personal views probably aligned best with the first group that wanted to keep moving forward as an independent nation.

Fred Fox – like George Washington – chose to have no political affiliation despite his personal leanings, and David thought that tradition was worth preserving.

Arriving back in Penndelom and stepping down from the helicopter, David chose to share a ride with the pilot back to the center of town. Then, he'd walk the final distance home.

Though the hour was already 9:00 pm, Jen knew David would be coming so she held supper until his arrival.

Unexpectedly warm in mid-fall, following the pattern set by an unusually hot summer, they ate and drank a glass of wine as David brought her up to date on events in Harrisburg, including news about the Peace Conference requested by the Harcastles.

Finishing his story with his guess that he'd get the support needed to commit PA to participate, David said that he would like to have Jen join him for that trip and suggested they take a walk through the streets of Penndelom now that the sun had set and the temperature had moderated a little bit to the high 60's.

The town was not picturesque, and little had changed over the past few years to soften the unfriendly stone and glass buildings that lined the streets. Nevertheless, David felt a comfortable sense of reassurance being back home . . . a feeling he'd seldom experienced in the capital.

Holding Jen's hand as they walked through various neighborhoods, David asked, "If you had to describe your vision of the ideal life, what would that be?"

"I suppose a life that provides moments like these – able to take a late-night walk through familiar streets without fear for our safety. You *do* know that news of the attempt on your life almost killed me. Even though I knew you were fine, that was one of the longest afternoons of my life, and I don't want to feel that way again."

"I'm so sorry you had to go through that," David responded and put his arm around her shoulder.

"Not your fault, but I don't want the kind of life for us that increases the likelihood of such moments. I don't want or need a high-profile world. My job doesn't really matter that much. I certainly want to feel satisfied and know that I am using my skills to contribute, but traditional measures of success – title, lots of money, and the like – just don't matter all that much anymore." She took a breath of the warmer than usual night air and continued, "So, does that answer your question about my ideal life? Or, were you really asking to get my opinion about our post-election life? Right now, I mostly care that we are together and prefer those days when we are not apart."

"That answers my question," David agreed. "People tell me I am apt to win the upcoming election, though I never submitted my name as a candidate. I continue to feel that I have only marginal control over my professional destiny."

Turning the corner. David and Jen saw the town's old brick elementary school.

"John O'Hara and I walked to that building every day for years, played in the school yard, and got ourselves ready for a future neither one of us could have ever foreseen. He was going to be a forest ranger, and I was going to be a famous athlete. Neither of us even came close to realizing those dreams."

Arriving back at their home after an hour-long walk, David and Jen sat on their small balcony and sipped wine.

Later – after a few rounds of passionate love making – David looked at Jen and smiled, enjoying the moment and his good fortune.

"Why aren't we married yet?" he asked.

"Because you haven't asked me," she teased, and then added more seriously, "No reason. No need. I feel pretty married."

"Me, too, but one of these days, we really should go ahead and get that done."

"Okay."

The next day, the phone rang early, and David got his go ahead to participate in the Round Table Peace Conference. He let the Harcastles know and asked whether any specific details had been decided – like when and where.

"If we want to pre-empt King, time is actually very tight," Jane noted, "so we've had to proceed with plans that assumed everything would work out. We are thinking 10 days from now, meeting in

Halifax, Nova Scotia. Nice neutral location, and they informally agreed to host. The event will last two days and involve a maximum of five participants per each of the four countries. We're looking to keep the group small in the hope of accomplishing big. Does that work for you David?"

"Yes. Security . . .?"

"Provided by Canada."

"Nice of them. I gave John O'Hara a preliminary heads-up call a few days ago. Nothing definitive obviously, but I have reason to believe they will be on board. What about Midwesterly?"

"I had a brief, early conversation with them the day before yesterday," Ben said. "At that time, they promised to attend but only if all three of the other countries were on board."

"Then, I'll look forward to seeing you in Halifax."

Nova Scotia Unity and Peace Conference

"So, Jen, we're off to Nova Scotia in a week."

"Sounds good. You know, David, I wouldn't really be shocked to find we like the place so much we wanted to stay! An island that is part of another country with a history of peace and neutrality and very scenic to boot. Plus, a port on the ocean. Who could ask for anything more?"

"Then, you better be sure to pack carefully."

"You think I'm kidding."

"No. I know you well enough to know better."

"Do you think King has gotten wind of the conference?"

"Guaranteed. He once had a large and very elaborate network of contacts, and he hasn't been away for so long. Some of that must still exist," he answered and then – seeming thoughtful, added, "I do hope the place is secure. These days, violence is so common you really can't take any chances, and King has very little to lose."

The trip to Halifax was uneventful. Jen and David arrived early enough to get settled into their room and do a little sightseeing.

A small city – by old U.S. standards – the town had many very quaint, scenic sections and was also a port on the Atlantic Ocean, which dictated many of the qualities Halifax had assumed over time. Large ships were easily accommodated, and the harbor also supported a nearby naval base.

Jen and David ended their excursion as tourists with a quick drink at a local pub before getting ready to meet the others from PA and the remaining countries for a kick-off dinner.

"Is Gretchen coming?" Jen asked, still feeling a twinge of jealousy and annoyed at herself for feeling that way.

"Yes. Perry is attending as our CRO, and Gretchen now works closely with him. Although she's never really gotten over Fred's assassination, she's landed on her feet."

"What does Perry have to say about the conference?"

"He's a supporter but a very skeptical one. He has spoken with Marcus Marovitch over the phone, but tonight will be his first meeting with the Harcastles. Apparently, no one knows yet who Midwesterly will be sending."

The evening went smoothly. King had unwittingly given all the attendees an issue that everyone without exception could agree upon – the need to keep King out of their futures. As a result, all conversation was amicable and seemed to generate a strong sense of fraternity . . . until Gretchen got word through some of PA's intelligence channels that King was planning some sort of initiative, the nature and scope of which was unknown.

Suddenly, all the attendees seemed edgy and started to look out for themselves and their delegations by returning almost immediately to their rooms.

"Doesn't take much to break through a thin veneer of fellowship," Gretchen observed.

"No," David responded. "This does not bode well for a permanent alliance among our countries. Still, as long as we present a unified front for enough time to discourage King, the trip and conference will have been well worthwhile."

Leaving, the four members of the PA delegation were the last to return from the restaurant to the hotel. Curious, David asked, "Perry, any guess about the disruption King has planned?"

"Not really, though I'm thinking low-tech. He lacks the resources and technical expertise to do otherwise."

"Well, get some sleep. We've got an early start," David reminded them.

The night passed uneventfully, and the meeting the next day got off to a smooth enough start. All four countries agreed to issue a statement to the press – choosing that to be their vehicle for sending King a message – that an act of aggression toward any of the four countries would be viewed as an act of aggression against all four of them and would be met with unified resistance.

Gretchen Moriority drafted the statement. The group agreed to some minor revisions, and the day ended with the document being sent to the press.

Part II of the Conference was scheduled to be devoted to the creation of a formal group and mutual defense treaty so the day's actions could become ongoing and be broader in scope.

Having spent the entire day together, the delegations went their separate ways for dinner.

As the PA group sat down at a table in the dining room of the hotel's restaurant, Gretchen handed David a message. "We've heard from King. Since I was the one to send out the statement," she said, "he apparently decided to use me for his response. No details were provided, but he sent one line that stated, "Please pass along my sympathies to the Widow June Harcastle."

"Well, we need to warn them that they are the target. Any idea where they went?" David asked.

"No, but I'll find out," Perry stated. He returned to their table a few minutes later. "I got word to the Northeasterly delegation about King's threat. They appreciated the heads up but seemed unsurprised."

"They are pretty cool customers," David agreed.

"They have no idea what King plans but will be especially careful," Perry concluded.

"What can we do?" David asked.

"Right now, not much," the CRO responded.

"King is not a subtle guy," David noted.

Taking the elevator to go back to their rooms for the night, David, Jen, Perry, and Gretchen stepped out and into the hall, as a person dressed as a bellhop stepped in – behaving nervously.

"Excuse me," David started to say to the person — when the bellhop burst out of the elevator and began racing down the stairs.

Everyone ran, but David moved fastest and caught up with the person on the stairs two flights down – tackling him with enough momentum that the two rolled an extra ten steps before coming to a stop on the sixth floor. The other three chasers were not far behind. Then, the four of them escorted the bellhop back up to the Northeasterly Suite and delivered their prize to Ben and June Harcastle.

After consulting the security detail assigned to the Conference, it turned out the man had planted a listening device in their room, as well as a small explosive in Ben's suitcase.

King was detained for questioning in his adopted country with extradition seeming extremely likely.

Upon notifying the other delegations, Midwesterly decided to pull out and head home – mission accomplished. With one country gone, the others had no reason to stay because the chance of achieving a formal treaty and mutual defense agreement had been lost.

Ben and June thanked the PA Delegation for their support and personal efforts, expressing regret over the lost opportunity but promising to be in touch.

Southwesterly left quickly, heading home to plot their own course into the future.

Glad that the threat of King was again gone – perhaps permanently, David also felt a key chance had been lost that might not come again for a very long time.

The four new countries appeared likely to further isolate themselves in figuring out a future that best served their individual self-interests.

However, David did believe PA no longer had to fear future annexation attempts from neighbors and could drop any discussion about becoming another country's territory.

Fred Fox would be glad.

He said as much to Perry, Gretchen, and Jen, adding, "So where does PA go from this point?"

"We try to get back on track with Fred's original plan I guess," Gretchen suggested.

"Though perhaps a bit modified," said Perry.

"Fred wanted self-sufficiency, but we've ended up with total isolationism. Seems likely that violence will resurface periodically as one country or another starts feeling cramped in small borders and looks for conquests."

"That's certainly history's lesson."

"You don't think we've learned better?" Jen asked.

"We can only hope," David responded, "while trying to do our part."

"Perry, the conference ended early, and everyone is clearing out, but I think Jen and I are going to stay the extra day as originally planned, do some sightseeing, get to know the area a little better, and check out a traditional Nova Scotia fishing village."

"Don't blame you."

"We'll see you back in Harrisburg in a few days."

"Enjoy," Perry said, and Jen responded, "We'll certainly do our best!"

While the conference had been a success in accomplishing the specific mission of stopping King's re-emergence, the abrupt end of the session without completing 'Day 2' seemed likely to set the tone for the foreseeable future.

While science and technology continued to exist, the kind of isolationism that characterized the past seemed unlikely. However, these disciplines probably would suffer as collaboration and the free sharing of information disappeared.

A considerable amount of time would no doubt pass before people lost the skills and knowledge to use and maintain their technology. Once that happened – then and only then – would a true second coming of an age of ignorance occur.

To David Evans, that appeared to be the heart of the matter. Being reduced in size and scope did not trouble him and did, in fact, seem preferable in many ways. He really could have contented himself within the confines of a totally independent Penndelom. However, small and isolated also appeared to him to come at a cost, and David did not believe that Fred Fox even contemplated that issue when he charted the current course for PA.

Sleepy streets, quiet neighborhoods, corner stores, town meetings, and small local school systems all seemed attractive to David, who could easily imagine each in a future Penndelom. However, he wondered whether Fred would have found that portrait appealing or whether he just assumed PA would eventually get bigger – in influence and importance if not land mass.

In many ways, Canada seemed to have done a better job than the more reckless U.S. at being big. When you crossed the border from one to the other at Niagara Falls, you could immediately see and feel the difference. The Canadian side was quieter, slower, cleaner, and less intrusive.

It was better than the place the United States had become after several unfortunate regimes had done their damage.

Could the newly divided states of America do better? Would these smaller, regional countries still be able to support an educational system that continued to promote scientific and cultural advances, or would they lack the drive and resources that had been the hallmark of the success of the U.S. during the golden years?

David had only questions – not answers.

"So, I'm thrilled we get to play hooky another day in Halifax," Jen said to David. "Or are we running away for good? If you just want to stay, I'm fine with that but wished I'd packed more clothes," she only half-teased.

"Well, we can look the place over," David offered, "just in case the future takes a wrong turn."

"You know they are going to be disappointed that you are not home campaigning with the election so close."

"I've done no campaigning and don't intend to start."

Buying fish and chips from a small stand and eating at a picnic table on the wharf, David looked out at the ocean and saw a large military vessel arriving at the port.

"Let them be disappointed. For the next 12 hours, we're tourists," he said.

"Marcus, we just wanted to call and thank you for attending the conference. Have you given any thought to a follow-up meeting?" Ben Harcastle asked.

"I'm afraid that will not be possible at the moment. In Southwesterly, the overwhelming sentiment of the day is to see what we can make of ourselves alone without being dragged down by other influences. I think people might be romanticizing the rugged individualism of the old west and imagining themselves as the logical successor to that crown," he concluded. "The timing is just all wrong, though I'm glad we were able to participate yesterday. A last hurrah."

"Us, too," June said, "and we thank you."

"Have you spoken with David yet?" Marcus asked.

"No. He apparently stayed behind another day."

"Business or pleasure?" Marcus asked. "Assuming he wins his election, which seems a safe bet, perhaps we can talk again at that point, though I suspect even that might be too soon. Still, David might be your key to getting everybody to agree to meet again."

"Perhaps," Ben conceded. "Guess we'll see, though Midwesterly probably needs some separate reason to come."

"Any chance David will lose the election?" Marcus asked.

"Normally, I'd say he's a shoo-in," Ben answered, "but the world no longer seems to be a predictable place."

The Election

With the election to name Fred Fox's replacement as the Chief Executive Officer of Pennsylvania just a week away, activities were heating up among the wannabes – which did not include David Evans. Though he was generally considered to be the head of the moderate party that sought to bring Fred Fox's dream to reality and was expected to win, the gap was narrowing.

Both Marianne Dragon, who ran under the conservative party that wanted to join Northeasterly, and Jeff Walker, who led an even more conservative group that wanted to reunite the U.S., had been campaigning very aggressively for many weeks. While the dynamics between PA and Northeasterly had changed since the Harcastles assumed power and the Peace Conference ended, Dragon still wanted PA to join a larger country – thereby eliminating responsibility for self-determination – a preferable place to be for many.

David, on the other hand, continued to refuse to campaign and contented himself with trying to be an adequate caretaker of the country while people made up their minds and cast their votes.

Increasingly, David had elected to spend his time in – and perform his duties from – Penndelom, which further removed him from the fray.

Since the abrupt conclusion of the Halifax Peace Conference, all the countries that had once comprised the United States seemed to have agreed as one to withdraw into themselves. Borders were closed, and even the trade of non-essential goods had been reduced to a trickle. On an individual level, real estate boomed as more and more properties were put up for sale – the owners apparently choosing to make permanent homes in different neighboring countries – often to be closer to family members.

The printing of money, previously a subject of only moderate interest, was becoming one of the key ways in which regime identities were being carved out. Open borders had once allowed the countries to continue to utilize and support the old currency. Post Peace Conference, those dollars devalued as each regional country created their own. Where most financial transactions had been paperless during the final chapters of the U.S.'s story, the new money returned to physical bills and coins – tangible symbols of the new independence and nationalism.

The Pennsylvania dollar bore the picture of Fred Fox.

"David, you can't assume that you can just sit in your office and expect to win," Gretchen Moriority warned him.

"I'm not," David retorted. "I'm sitting in Penndelom."

"Ha. Ha," she said.

"Gretchen's right," Perry interjected. "Can you imagine where we'll be should either of those crackpots win?"

"What's the latest news on the incentive?" David asked to change the subject.

"They were finally activated earlier this week. Quite a few applicants appear to be willing to try their hands at farming and manufacturing," Gretchen answered.

"Of course, they won't know what they are doing," Perry added. "So, I expect we'll see a high incidence of failure."

"Maybe at first, "David said, "but they are willing to at least try, and that has to count for something."

David found himself retreating more and more frequently to Penndelom as election day drew closer and closer. In his hometown, David was still able to walk the streets without being accosted by people feeling compelled to share their political views with him.

On this particular night, he and Jen had eaten a quiet supper and were now out for some fresh air.

"Harrisburg tomorrow?" Jen asked.

"Yes." David replied.

"Are they still trying to get you to debate?"

"Yes."

"And you keep refusing?" Jen stated but with her voice rising to suggest a question.

"Yes. However, I have agreed to hold a town meeting that can be broadcast across the Internet."

"They must have been pleased by that!"

"Once the election is over, I do hope that everyone will be better able to concentrate on the job at hand – trying to build a country. The people who want a new United States don't seem to get that a return to the past will never happen. We couldn't even get all parties to stay for 'Day 2' of the conference much less reunite these disparate views."

Pennsylvania may be allowed to join Northeasterly, which would probably happen under pretty favorable terms – especially under the Harcastles. David could imagine much worse outcomes than being part of their nearest neighbor. However, that neighbor was already under a second regime . . . so you had to wonder about the strength and stability of the current government. Completing that thought process, David wondered aloud to Jen, "While I think Dragon's group might ultimately be right, I think their reasons for wanting to be part of Northeasterly are the wrong ones."

"So," Jen said, "you better make sure you and the moderates win the election next Tuesday."

"I'm really not right for that job in almost every way, and you and I don't really relish the lifestyle."

"But you *do* have a strong sense of duty," she reminded him.

"Let's change the subject and enjoy the night before I get depressed. We'll be back at the capital tomorrow."

"Well, David," you somehow managed to get through the whole town meeting without mentioning the election or campaigning," Gretchen observed. "I admit the conversation about incentives and the creation of new industries, as well as the discussion about the state of PA's finances and currency are important, but Tuesday's vote matters, too."

"I've still never agreed that I'm running. Everyone seems to assume that's the case, but I never formally declared my intention and willingness."

"Well, the pundits have started speculating that Perry will be your running mate as COO."

"And a fine selection he would be because that would guarantee your continued involvement in a significant role."

"Which just makes me jump for joy," Gretchen responded sarcastically.

"You're a lifer; you know you are," David countered.

"Somebody has to be willing," she conceded. "You do realize that fate keeps placing you in the way of history. Chances are, you'll never again be allowed to retreat into your shell."

"I don't know about that. You do remember that our elections were set up for people to vote for the party – not the person. Probably a reaction at the time to the fact that Fred had just been assassinated. Anyway, people don't vote for Jeff Walker; they vote for the Patriot Party. Then, the Party appoints or anoints the individual to lead the party. Generally speaking, that will have happened in advance."

On the eve of the election – while Marianne Dragon and Jeff Walker were out campaigning – David met with the people from manufacturing and agriculture to monitor the progress of the new incentive program designed to stimulate growth in these needed areas.

Jen, too, had a packed schedule and had been assigned to prepare materials to get news coverage for that initiative.

When their days were done, they boarded a helicopter for a flight back to Penndelom. Though they'd probably be heading to Harrisburg again the day after tomorrow, David wanted to be home for election day.

David and Jen walked to the official polling place the next morning. As they entered the school, they had to pass through several groups of supporters, including his own, who were making last minute pitches to secure votes.

After having their names taken by several elderly ladies handling the registration table, they were offered coffee and homemade cookies while waiting their turn.

"That's the real reason I wanted to come home to vote," joked David. "The cookies!"

They then wandered down the hall looking at photos and a trophy case. When their names were called, they moved forward to their respective machines and cast their votes, leaving by a different door at the back of the building.

"Any surprises in the way you voted?" Jen asked.

"Secret ballot. I can't tell."

Back in their apartment, Jen said, "You know, I really did seriously consider staying in Halifax. I tried to imagine what life would be like. Didn't seem too bad to me," she said with a smile and then asked, "When you've talked about walking away from the political life we've been leading, have you been serious about that alternative?"

"More than you'd probably imagine," he said.

Jen then remarked, "I never found politics to be particularly fascinating but always hoped to get a job that I found interesting. To date, none of my roles have been ideal."

"So, what would your perfect job be?"

"Then or now?" she asked for clarification.

"Both."

"Then – a fashion model or movie star," she quipped. "Now – a fashion model or movie star."

"Seriously," he urged.

"Back then – I probably pictured myself writing for a magazine, though I had only the vaguest notion of all that was involved. Now – I think I just want a job that will allow me enough time and money to live my life the way I want. I suppose I still prefer to deal with words but would also be happy doing that as an avocation on the side if – for instance – I was able to start my own business. What about you, David?"

"That is the question," he stated. "Maybe my job should be doing whatever might be necessary to support your ambitions."

He then changed the subject by silently leading her in the direction of their bedroom.

By 5:00 pm, enough ballots had been cast and tabulated to project a Moderate Party – led by David Evans – victory. David Evans had been a clear winner.

By 6:00 pm, Walker had conceded.

By 7:00 pm, Dragon conceded as well.

By 8:00 pm, everyone was calling for David to make his acceptance speech.

By 9:00 pm, David – with the help of Jen – had drafted his statement and stepped to the podium at the high school gym where the votes had been cast and counted.

"On behalf of the Moderate Party, I thank you for the overwhelming vote of confidence you have provided today. As you know, the Moderate Party provides a clear link back to our recent past and represents a commitment to fulfilling Fred Fox's dream of a totally independent Pennsylvania free from having to make compromises to build coalitions – which is the typical fate of larger countries and governments.

"While I have been very proud to be part of PA's history during this momentous time, I am choosing to step away from leading the party and place you in the very capable hands of Perry Adams, who is far better equipped than me for the job ahead."

The crowd grew silent.

Not a sound was heard in the gym, until someone finally stated, "No. You can't just walk away."

"I pledge," David continued, "to work closely with Perry Adams in making a smooth transition. He will also be assisted by Gretchen Moriority – former alter ego of Fred Fox – and a very capable and experienced staff.

"I want them to succeed. My future is also in their hands, so rest assured my successor will have any help required of me. I'll be nearby. I'm planning to stay in Penndelom."

Glancing across at Jen, he gained confidence from her smile. They'd had enough conversations about such a decision that he was certain he knew where her head and heart would be.

Stepping back from the podium, David spoke with a technician. His remarks had been broadcast back to Harrisburg and across the state. Now, he officially passed the gavel by stating, "Perry Adams would like to have a word with you. While we don't have a jumbotron, his remarks will be piped through the loudspeaker from Harrisburg where he's been listening to my comments and is about to address the crowd that has gathered.

David felt his phone vibrate in his pocket and saw a text message from Gretchen had arrived, "You're really going to do this?"

Then, another from John O'Hara followed, "Good for you. Come live in Southwesterly; you'd fit right in."

"As you know," Perry began, "David Evans will never cease to surprise us – always doing the unexpected – whether that involves turning up in unexpected places or charting an unexpected course. I appreciate his confidence in me and my staff and gladly accept the challenge of helping PA move forward into the future while taking the next step.

"When David promises to make himself available to us going forward, I don't doubt that he will be as good as his word. Let's wish him well with his next endeavor while sincerely thanking him for his countless contributions to our successes over the past several years."

Initially, quiet applause greeted these remarks from a stunned audience, but the clamor gradually swelled to a state of pandemonium with countless gestures of encouragement as Perry Adams concluded his speech.

David waved and walked across the stage to Jen and said, "The deed is done."

"I'm proud of you. Stepping aside couldn't have been easy. Time for us to get on with our lives."

That night, David and Jen took a slow walk home – glad to be in the familiar friendly surrounds of Penndelom.

The transition began the day after the election. David and Jen flew back to Harrisburg that morning. Since David had never chosen to change his office and occupy Fred's CEO Suite, no physical move was required, and he had time during the upcoming weeks to gather up his small number of personal belongings and vacate the premises.

David and Jen decided to just keep their small convenience apartment because they chose to commute back and forth from Penndelom, so no change was required until the lease ran out in a month.

Perry, not surprisingly, chose to settle into the office and official home of the PA CEO, so Fred's widow was in the process of finding a new place.

In his own mind, David was giving Perry a full month before clearing out and just remaining on call. If Perry wanted, less time would be fine. He very much doubted that he would want David hanging around more than that.

Although Perry had met Marcus Marovitch and Ben and June Harcastle, David set up formal teleconferences with them over the next couple of weeks as much for them as for Perry.

David made sure Gretchen Moriarty was included in each session. For he was quite certain that she – more than Perry or him – was the key to standing a chance to realize Fred Fox's vision for PA. She had the clearest understanding of his goal and the best grasp of the obstacles that stood in the way. Perry would be a good caretaker for a few years, but Gretchen was the soul and did not let personal ambitions cloud her judgement.

David vowed to do all in his power to assist her in any way across time. For he was quite certain for some unknown reason that she was destined to be a bit of a fixture in Jen and his life for the duration – periodically turning up at key moments in a way likely to cause them to change course or, perhaps more accurately, stay on course.

Why was he so convinced?

He did not know, but certainly his experiences to date bore that out.

"So, you really went and did this thing," Gretchen said to him one day. "In the end, I was convinced you wouldn't. I know you have a strong sense of duty."

"PA will be in good hands with Perry."

"Different hands," Gretchen noted, "that's for sure. Perry Adams has a very different way of conducting business – much more formal and traditional."

"Which may be a good change," David noted. "The country is growing up. We're past that early stage so a bit more structure and formality will probably be healthy and get us taken more seriously. Besides, Perry, too, will only be around for just so long until he also gives way to a successor."

"That's a stretch," Gretchen responded. "David, you will be missed."

Jen, too, had decided to give up her role as a press secretary on the communications staff. Frankly, her job had never been the same or as interesting with Fred Fox gone. He had used her skills differently, and she felt she'd had a place in shaping policy, not just reporting on decisions that had already been made.

To avoid any hint of favoritism, David and Jen had elected to work directly together very infrequently. So, her duties largely shifted from the executive office, which she preferred, to other needs. Besides, David made less use of the government's media team than Fred had.

Nevertheless, Jen's presence had been a big one within her department – most of whom had written David comic hate mail upon learning that he'd be taking her away from them.

Jen did not expect Perry Adams to use the press as successfully as Fred Fox, though she suspected he would try to use them more than David had. In the end, she had very few regrets about leaving her job. However, she knew she'd miss the people. Unlike David, she had a knack for forming many deep and lasting relationships in a very short time.

David did stay actively involved in the launch of the manufacturing and agricultural incentive program, which he continued to see as key, throughout the month. However, he soon felt that each had gotten off to about as good a start as one could reasonably expect . . . so, he felt free of that responsibility well within the deadlines he had established for himself.

Meanwhile, the world grew more closed and isolated. The four countries had now all shut down their borders, which increasingly eliminated casual interactions. The shift of people from one country to another started to slow down as people made arrangements to relocate to their long-range permanent home base.

While technology still existed and allowed the financial structure of society to keep functioning, new innovations within the scientific community were rare with interactions among developers virtually non-existent.

After a brief vacation in Nova Scotia, David and Jen set about the task of structuring their new life.

Neither of them had any regrets.

They settled back into a quiet existence in Penndelom. Shortly after returning, they gave up their apartments and bought a house together. Jen took a job with the local newspaper, and David started substitute teaching while looking for a more permanent solution.

Although John O'Hara continued to approach him with some very tempting offers to relocate to Southwesterly, David ultimately felt he had an east coast personality and refused. The two stayed in close touch, though, and John periodically mentioned – jokingly by now – that he'd like to have his dog back.

David informally consulted with Ben and June Harcastle from time to time. Northeasterly immediately prospered under their guidance, and they remained interested in getting PA to voluntarily join, but events did not allow for that. With the influence of Fred Fox continuing to be strong in PA, such a merger of fortunes was unlikely.

Life had hit a comfortable rhythm, and David and Jen could have happily been swept along for a very long time, but events did not cooperate. Just as he had once found himself carrying a new flag on stage in Penndelom and later, a major part of the storyline when an assassin changed the course of PA history, David – once again and through no fault or action of his own – found himself stuck in the middle of a key moment likely to change the arc of the future.

Looking Backward

The world had changed over the dozen years since David chose not to become the newly elected CEO of Pennsylvania. He'd opted to place the future of this Keystone country into the hands of former Chief Risk Officer Perry Adams — believing the citizens of PA would be in the care of someone better equipped to deal with the challenges faced by the new nation.

A Dozen Years Later

Pennsylvania had survived as an independent country but had not really thrived. Following Fred Fox's paradigm, PA had become more self-sufficient but in a state of poverty and crime not previously experienced as part of the United States. Unfortunately, small battles and skirmishes were an aspect of daily life along the borders.

The Current Map

Various countries made overtures to annex PA about every three years — first Northeasterly by force prior to the Harcastles, then Southwesterly via diplomacy/treaty, and finally Midwesterly by an invasion foiled largely through the help of Canada, which historically was known for neutrality and an unwillingness to take sides.

As for the Southeast and Deep South states, they, too, talked continuously about forming their own separate country but never managed to achieve sufficient consensus. Since none of those states were willing or able to go forward alone, each spent countless hours in discussion but eventually settled for finding a place within the other countries — especially Southwesterly. Florida and the Carolinas, however, chose to become geographical anomalies in Northeasterly. Although they were physically far apart from the rest of the region, the leadership recognized that much of the population in these jurisdictions had roots and philosophical/cultural ties to the Northeast.

David and Jen

During this decade, David resurfaced periodically as needed. For some reason, he never had to decide to become involved in a moment. Instead, the moment involved him.

That said, David and Jen lived a largely quiet life in Penndelom that was occasionally punctuated by a random high-profile reintroduction to the world. They bought a house, got married, had one child, and were expecting another. Jen carved out a career writing – gaining a reputation as a biographer and autobiographical ghostwriter. Her first great success was the story of Fred Fox's life. However, she also published books about the Harcastles, treated as a love story, and Marcus Marovitch. In addition, she taught a college writing course on the side. David, on the other hand, worked largely as a consultant in operations – his specialty – to various regional governments. As a wedding present, David and Jen were given a small parcel of land near Nova Scotia, and they were gradually able to add a small cottage – thanks in part to Jen's Fred Fox bio royalty checks.

As the conflicts between neighboring countries escalated in frequency and severity, David and Jen found themselves spending more and more time in Canada, though Penndelom seemed to have some sort of a hold on them that could not be ignored.

Penndelom

Penndelom gradually changed, too – a transformation seen through an evolving landscape. Stark stone buildings were softened by newer, smaller structures of wood and brick. Many people had planted trees, which had grown and matured enough to make a tangible difference in the atmosphere of the town. Streetlights – previously high, modern, mercury-based lamps that cast a stark, flat glow were replaced by softer yellower, incandescent-like lights.

Some of the credit had to be assigned to initiatives taken by the local university housed in the town.

Previously a small, two-year school, the college flourished as PA became independent and more and more students opted to stay closer to home and also take advantage of financial incentives to remain in the same country – benefitting the educational institution greatly. One of the leaders of that transformation was a new outspoken President named Dr. Garth Payne – a PA native who returned from Midwesterly with his wife, along with their son and his family, to lead the school through a new chapter of growth.

Epilogue

One of the first times David re-entered the public arena was prompted by a visit to the campus by the Harcastles. Although they had always been friends to Pennsylvania, Northeasterly had not, and they were greeted by a large angry group of protesters who had formed a line – creating a barrier – outside the main entrance to the campus.

Having received an S.O.S. from June Harcastle, David agreed to meet them and accompany them to their destination.

In PA, especially Penndelom, David Evans had achieved a certain folk hero status. In people's minds, he was associated with much that was good that happened in Penndelom after secession from the United States.

Although David tended to feel like a fraud who hadn't earned such popular status, he nevertheless had a deep sense of loyalty to the place and to those individuals who – like the Harcastles – he counted as among a select group of friends.

With David leading the way, the protestors grew silent, and a space opened for the Harcastles to pass through.

Greeting the group, the President of the University introduced Ben and June but handed the microphone to David before allowing the visitors to speak. "Sorry. I did not come prepared," he stated, honest and straightforward as always. "I came because Ben and June Harcastle have always been our ally and very helpful to PA, Penndelom, and me personally; so, I was pleased to have a chance to show off our little town, this great university, and hopefully help promote future bonds of friendship between our countries."

With that, he handed the mic to June, who simply said, "Thank you, David. We've come to Pennsylvania to pledge our support in your continued struggle to maintain independence. While we regret your decision not to become part of Northeasterly, we are aware that other countries would like to annex you – perhaps using whatever forceful means are available. We came to pledge our resources to defend your right to independence. We chose to come to Penndelom to make that commitment because your town is the place that shook the world, that started the string of secessions that marked the beginning of the downfall of the old United States and the last — and worst — president of that empire: ex-President King.

"David Evans was in attendance that day many years ago to present Penndelom's new flag to the world. We wanted him to be on hand on the day we commit to working with you to preserve that freedom."

"Thank you, June," David said in response. "Know that we would do the same for you."

While this event ended up being a quiet moment – the kind unlikely to make the history books, the actions on this day made history because of a subsequent event that did *not* occur.

Faced with the prospect of going to war with Northeasterly, a planned attack on PA by Midwesterly was postponed – an initiative that would not turn up again for another half dozen or so years.

Did David's presence make a difference that day at the campus? Although he'd say it hadn't, popular opinion would generally disagree with him.

David had a knack for turning up at public events or finding himself in the midst of national activities at the climactic moment – always refusing any kind of formal role and turning down any offers that came his way.

While Jen sometimes wondered whether he was selling himself short, she also recognized that his personality created his effectiveness and had been around him long enough to know that much of their future – his, hers, and their family's – was still to be written and fully expected that, wanted or not, exciting times would be finding them again.

Acknowledgements

Special thanks to my editors Abby Macenka and Penny Dowden as well as to my own special group of beta readers: Molly, Judy, Dylan, Caitlin, Carole, and Carroll (plus Ruthie, of course, in spirit and in absentia).

A lifelong love of the written word first led Bob to a professional career in communications. During a tenure that began with a small, de novo operation, Bob oversaw all aspects from advertising, web development, and public relations to more technical editorial tasks, but the written word was always the common denominator. Recently, he co-authored a blog, which has been on hiatus the past two years while Bob pursued his early love of fiction and completed his novel Divided States.

Bob and his wife Molly have two adult children, Caitlin and Dylan, which became three with the addition of Dylan's wife Kelly. Bob and Molly split time between Dallas and Harvey's Lake in Pennsylvania. He is a graduate of Bucknell University.

www.ingramcontent.com/pod-product-compliance
Lightning Source LLC
Chambersburg PA
CBHW010559310726
48969CB00009B/2487